Table of C

The Bloodborn Chronicles (The the Queen, #6)...
   1. The Queen's Descent 7
   2. The Betrayer's Whisper 21
   3. The Crimson Court 31
   4. A Legacy of Blood..43
   1. Vanguard's Return 59
   2. The Witch's Mark..73
   3. Into the Abyss 89
   4. Alliances of Blood 106
   1. The War of Shadows 123
   2. The Price of Power 139
   3. The Queen's Choice 155
   4. The Crimson Dawn 171
Epilogue: A New Dawn 185

THE BLOODBORN CHRONICLES

THE LAST RECKONING

SERIES: "THE BLOODBORN CHRONICLES: RISE OF THE QUEEN"

BOOK 6

DORIAN VALE

Copyright © 2025 Dorian Vale

"Every man has his secret sorrows which the world knows not."
– Henry Wadsworth Longfellow

The Bloodborn Chronicles

The Last Reckoning

Book 6
of the series:
"The Bloodborn Chronicles: Rise of the Queen"

Part I: The Awakening of Shadows

1. The Queen's Descent

○ The Return of Elara

Elara stood at the edge of the cliff, the wind whipping through her dark hair, pulling it into wild tendrils that seemed to mirror the chaos within her heart. Below, the kingdom stretched out, shrouded in mist and sorrow, as if even the land itself mourned her return. It had been years—years since she had walked away from the throne, years since her name had been uttered in whispers of both reverence and fear. But now, the blood of the old kings called to her, as undeniable as the pull of the moon on the tides.

The journey had been long, fraught with peril. She had crossed deserts where the sun scorched the earth, ventured through forests haunted by creatures born of nightmare, and braved mountains that touched the very heavens. But none of it had been as difficult as what lay ahead—returning to a land she had once ruled with a firm but fair hand, now broken and torn by time and betrayal.

Her eyes narrowed as she scanned the horizon, her sharp gaze catching the gleam of the distant castle. The walls that once held the laughter of children and the wisdom of her ancestors now stood silent, cold, and unwelcoming. The people had forgotten her—if they ever truly remembered who she was. To them, she was a legend, a shadow of the past, a queen who had abandoned them when they needed her the most.

But Elara knew better. Her departure had not been of her own choosing. It had been forced upon her by powers that she could no longer ignore. Forces beyond her control had conspired to strip her of everything she had fought for—her throne, her family, her very identity.

Now, the time had come to reclaim it all. But the path was fraught with dangers both old and new. There were those who would seek to use her return to their advantage, those who would see her dead, and those who would seek to manipulate the power she possessed. The bloodline of the Bloodborn was not one to be trifled with, and she was their rightful heir.

Yet, as Elara turned away from the cliff and began the long descent back to the heart of her kingdom, a weight settled on her chest. The power she wielded was not the same as it had been before. The years of exile had shaped her in ways she could not have anticipated, and the woman who would return to the throne was not the same as the girl who had once ruled with youthful idealism. She had learned the cost of power, the price of leadership, and the terrible toll it could take on the soul.

But she would not falter. Not now. Not when the kingdom needed her most.

As Elara approached the gates of her home, a sense of dread mingled with determination. She knew that her return would not be greeted with open arms, that many would question her right to lead. But the blood of the kings ran through her veins, and she would not allow anyone to forget that.

The gates creaked open slowly, the sound echoing through the stillness like the moan of a dying world. And as Elara stepped across the threshold, she was met not by cheers or adulation, but by a chilling silence—a silence that spoke volumes.

The kingdom had changed. And so had she.

But Elara would see it rise again, no matter the cost.

The streets that had once echoed with the laughter of children and the bustling of market vendors were now eerily quiet. The banners that once fluttered proudly from every corner had long since withered, their once-vibrant colors faded and torn. Elara's boots, heavy with the weight of her journey, echoed loudly on the cobblestone roads as she made her way deeper into the heart of the city.

A sense of foreboding clung to the air like a thick fog, and Elara could feel the eyes of the people upon her—eyes filled not with warmth or recognition, but with suspicion. They had heard the stories, the rumors that had spread like wildfire in her absence. Some believed her to be dead, others whispered that she had betrayed her people, and there were those who still clung to the hope that the queen they had once known would return to lead them once more.

As Elara passed by the homes and shops, she could see the hollowed-out expressions of the kingdom's citizens. Their faces were gaunt, their eyes tired and haunted. The once-thriving kingdom was now little more than a shell of what it had been, its people broken, its soul shattered. Her heart ached for them, for what they had endured in her absence.

She continued, her steps unflinching, her mind focused on the task at hand. There was no room for sentimentality. Not now. Not when there was so much to be done.

The grand hall of the castle loomed ahead, its towering spires and battlements casting long shadows over the city. As Elara approached the gates, she could feel the weight of her lineage pressing down on her, the legacy of the Bloodborn coursing through her veins, calling her to reclaim what was rightfully hers.

The guards at the castle gates did not recognize her at first. They stood in her way, their armor gleaming in the dim light of the evening, their faces stern and unyielding.

"Halt!" one of them barked. "Who goes there?"

Elara's voice was steady, her tone unshakable as she replied, "It is I—Elara, Queen of the Bloodborn, rightful heir to the throne of this kingdom."

The guards exchanged uncertain glances, their hands resting on the hilts of their swords. The weight of Elara's words seemed to hang in the air, but the disbelief on their faces was palpable.

"Elara? You... you are alive?" one of the guards muttered, his voice tinged with both disbelief and fear.

Elara did not flinch. "I am alive. And I am here to reclaim my kingdom."

With a hesitant motion, one of the guards stepped aside, allowing Elara to pass. As she entered the castle, the cold stone walls seemed to close in on her, the silence overwhelming. The once-immense halls were now empty, their grandeur lost to time and neglect. She could feel the weight of history pressing down on her shoulders, each step forward a reminder of the burden she had long carried.

But this was her destiny. This was what she had been born for.

As Elara made her way through the castle, she was keenly aware of the absence of those who should have been there—her advisors, her generals, the people who had once stood by her side. It was as if they, too, had vanished into the shadows of the past.

Finally, she reached the throne room, its massive doors creaking open as she stepped inside. The room that had once been filled with the sound of her voice, issuing commands and decrees, was now silent. The throne, once a symbol of her power, sat empty, shrouded in dust and neglect.

Elara's heart clenched as she approached it. The weight of the seat seemed almost unbearable now, its emptiness echoing the void she had felt for so long.

But she did not hesitate. She would not be cowed by the memories of her past, nor by the uncertainty of her future. She had come back, and she would see her kingdom restored.

Taking a deep breath, Elara sat down on the throne, feeling the cold stone beneath her. The room seemed to come alive with the weight of her presence, the shadows of the past shifting around her like whispers in the dark.

It was time. Time to reclaim what was hers. Time to fight for the future of the kingdom, and for the bloodline of the Bloodborn.

The road ahead would not be easy. The enemies she had once trusted, the ones who had plotted against her, were still out there. And the kingdom was not the same as it had been before. It was fractured, torn by factions, and filled with those who would stop at nothing to see her fail.

But Elara had faced worse. And she would not allow the kingdom to fall again.

She would rise.

And so would they.

The Return of Elara had begun.

○ A Kingdom on the Brink

The sun hung low over the horizon, casting long shadows across the desolate landscape. The kingdom, once proud and vibrant, now stood on the edge of ruin. The streets of the capital, once alive with laughter and bustling markets, now echoed with silence. There was an unsettling stillness in the air, as though the very earth itself was holding its breath, waiting for something catastrophic to unfold.

Elara stood at the balcony of the royal palace, her gaze fixed on the city below. Her once regal composure was now laced with doubt. The weight of her crown seemed heavier with every passing day, and the responsibilities it carried felt more like chains than symbols of power. She could feel the tension in the air, thick and suffocating. It was as though the kingdom itself was teetering on the brink of something darker—something beyond her control.

Whispers had spread like wildfire through the streets. Rumors of a new uprising, of a rebellion rising in the shadows, had begun to surface. There were those who believed that her rule had weakened the kingdom, that she had betrayed her ancestors by making deals with foreign powers, and that the Bloodborn curse had claimed her family. Others simply feared the growing unrest, the increasing tension between the noble houses, and the disillusionment of the common folk.

Elara's fingers tightened around the stone railing, her nails digging into the rough surface as she tried to steady her thoughts. She had never asked for this—never wanted the throne. But it had been thrust upon her after her father's untimely death, and now she was left to pick up the pieces of a crumbling empire. She had always tried to do what was best for her people, but the shadows that loomed over her reign seemed insurmountable.

Her thoughts were interrupted by a voice from behind her.

"Elara, you cannot stand here forever," came the voice of Rhiannon, her closest advisor and confidante. Rhiannon was a woman of rare wisdom, her eyes sharp and her words always carefully measured. She had been by Elara's side since the day of her father's death, guiding her through the treacherous waters of court politics.

Elara turned slowly, her eyes meeting Rhiannon's with a mixture of exhaustion and frustration. "I can feel it, Rhiannon," she whispered. "The kingdom is slipping away from me. I'm losing control."

Rhiannon stepped closer, her presence a calm in the storm. "You are not losing control," she said softly. "But the kingdom is in turmoil. There are forces at work—forces you may not fully understand. You must prepare yourself, Elara. The truth about your family's bloodline is more dangerous than you think."

Elara's heart sank at the mention of the bloodline. Her ancestors had ruled the kingdom for generations, but with their power came a dark legacy—the Bloodborn curse. It was said that the rulers of her family were born with extraordinary powers, but those powers came at a terrible cost. The curse had claimed the lives of many before her, and Elara feared that it would claim hers as well.

"I cannot ignore what's happening around me, Rhiannon," Elara replied, her voice trembling with a mixture of fear and resolve. "The people are angry, and they want change. They believe I am the cause of their suffering."

"Then we must act quickly," Rhiannon said, her tone sharp. "There are forces working against you from within the kingdom—traitors who seek to tear it apart. You must uncover their plans before it's too late."

Elara nodded slowly, her mind racing with thoughts of the task ahead. There was no time to waste. If she was to save her kingdom, she would have to confront the shadows that had long haunted her family—and face the truth of her bloodline.

The kingdom was on the brink, and the time for hesitation had passed. The question now was whether Elara had the strength to hold it together, or whether the weight of the crown would crush her beneath it.

As the evening light faded, casting a blood-red glow over the kingdom, Elara knew one thing for certain: the reckoning was coming, and it would change everything.

The moon rose high over the kingdom, its pale light casting an eerie glow over the palace walls. Elara paced back and forth in the royal chambers, her mind a whirlpool of uncertainty and fear. The weight of the decisions before her pressed heavily on her chest. If the kingdom was truly on the brink, there was no time left for hesitation. She had to act—now.

Rhiannon had left her to think, allowing her a few moments of solitude to gather her thoughts. But the silence was suffocating. Every shadow seemed to whisper threats, every creak of the old palace seemed like a distant echo of the kingdom's impending doom. Elara knew the stakes were higher than ever before. If she failed, everything she had known—her family, her kingdom—would crumble under the weight of betrayal and uprising.

Suddenly, the door to her chambers opened with a soft creak, and a figure stepped inside. It was Leander, the captain of the royal guard, his face grave and worn from sleepless nights. Elara's heart skipped a beat as she looked at him. He had always been her protector, her unwavering ally. His loyalty to her family was unquestionable, and yet there was something in his eyes tonight that unsettled her.

"Your Majesty," he said, bowing low before her. "There is news."

Elara's pulse quickened. "What news?" she demanded, her voice sharper than she intended.

Leander straightened, his brow furrowed. "The rebellion is not just a rumor, Elara. We've discovered that it's already in motion. The rebels have allies within the palace walls. Some of your own councilors, even members of the royal family, are said to be involved."

Her breath caught in her throat. The thought of traitors within her inner circle was enough to send a chill through her veins. She had always trusted those closest to her, but now doubt seeped into every corner of her mind. Who could she trust? Who among them was working against her?

"Who?" Elara asked, her voice trembling with a mix of disbelief and anger. "Who is leading this?"

Leander hesitated, his eyes flickering toward the door as though to make sure they were alone. "The leader is unknown, but there are whispers. The House of Valis is heavily implicated. Lord Kaelen Valis—he's been seen meeting with known dissidents. There's talk of him rallying support among the nobles."

Elara's stomach twisted at the mention of Lord Kaelen's name. He was one of the most influential figures in the kingdom, known for his sharp political mind and vast wealth. His family had always been a powerful force in the court, and if he had indeed aligned himself with the rebels, it would be a devastating blow to her rule.

"Lord Kaelen," she whispered under her breath, her mind racing. "I should have known. He has always coveted power."

Leander nodded grimly. "We need to act quickly, Your Majesty. The rebellion is gaining momentum, and if we don't make a move soon, it may be too late to stop them."

Elara's thoughts raced, trying to formulate a plan. The kingdom was in chaos, and her family's bloodline—the very thing that had once been their strength—was now a double-edged sword. She knew that if she didn't confront the growing rebellion soon, there would be no turning back.

But how could she strike at the heart of the rebellion when she couldn't even trust those closest to her?

"I will speak to Rhiannon," Elara said, her voice steady despite the turmoil in her chest. "We will find out who is behind this, and we will stop them. But we must move quietly. The fewer people know our intentions, the better."

Leander gave a respectful nod. "As you wish, Your Majesty. I will inform the guard and ensure that no one is alerted to our plans."

As Leander turned to leave, Elara's gaze lingered on him for a moment longer than usual. There was something in his expression—a glint of something she couldn't quite place. Was it worry? Or was it something else? She couldn't be sure.

When he was gone, Elara returned to the balcony, looking out over the kingdom. The once-proud city now seemed like a fragile shell, teetering on the edge of destruction. The rebellion had begun, and her throne—her very life—was at risk. She could feel the weight of it all pressing down on her, but there was no room for fear. She would have to fight for her crown, for her people, for her very survival.

A storm was coming. And Elara would stand against it, even if it meant facing the darkest corners of her kingdom—and her bloodline.

The night stretched on, and with it, the tension in the air thickened. Every hour brought them closer to the inevitable clash. The kingdom was on the brink, and Elara had no choice but to rise to meet the challenge, no matter the cost.

○ The Prophecy of the Bloodborn

In the quiet chambers of the ancient citadel, Elara stood before the weathered stone tablet, her fingers tracing the cryptic symbols carved into its surface. The air around her seemed thick with anticipation, as if the very walls of the castle were holding their breath. The prophecy, long buried in the shadows of forgotten time, was now coming to light once more.

The Bloodborn were not merely a legend. They were the embodiment of power, a bloodline that had once ruled the kingdom with an iron fist, their legacy hidden beneath the weight of centuries. The prophecy spoke of a time when the last of the Bloodborn would return, not to restore peace, but to ignite a war that would sweep across the lands, reshaping the world forever.

"Elara," a voice interrupted her thoughts. She turned to see Rhiannon, the kingdom's seer, standing in the doorway. Her eyes, usually sharp with wisdom, now held a shadow of doubt. "The prophecy... it's not what we expected."

Elara's heart skipped a beat. Rhiannon had been her most trusted ally, a woman whose visions had guided her through many a storm. But even Rhiannon seemed uncertain now, and that troubled her more than words could express.

"What does it say?" Elara asked, her voice a whisper, as if the very air might shatter the moment the words were spoken.

Rhiannon stepped forward, holding an ancient scroll in her hands. She unrolled it with care, as if the paper itself might disintegrate from the weight of history. "The Bloodborn will rise from the ashes of the old kingdom," she began, her voice steady but heavy with the gravity of the message. "Their return will bring both ruin and salvation, but not all who bear their blood will be allies. There is betrayal in the veins of their kin, and those who seek to wield their power will find themselves consumed by it."

Elara's brow furrowed. She had heard whispers of betrayal before, but this—this was something different. "Are you telling me that someone among us will betray the Bloodborn? That my bloodline is tainted?"

Rhiannon's gaze softened. "It's not a question of taint, Elara. It's a question of power. The Bloodborn are powerful, yes, but their power comes at a price. Each generation that bears their blood carries the weight of what came before—both the good and the bad. And as the prophecy warns, not every Bloodborn will be able to control the force that resides within."

Elara stepped back, her mind racing. She had always known there was more to her heritage than met the eye, but this? This was beyond anything she had ever imagined. The Bloodborn were meant to be the saviors of the kingdom, not its destroyers.

"What does it mean for me, then?" Elara asked, her voice barely a whisper. "Am I destined to fail? Am I to bring about the ruin that this prophecy speaks of?"

Rhiannon shook her head. "No. The prophecy speaks of a choice. A choice that will be made when the Bloodborn finally come into their full power. The question is not whether you can control it—it's whether you're willing to make the sacrifice that will be required to do so."

Elara felt a chill run down her spine. Sacrifice. She had heard the word before, but now it felt real, like an impending shadow looming over her future. What sacrifice could possibly be great enough to harness such a power without unleashing the destruction foretold?

"I don't know if I can do it," Elara admitted, her voice trembling.

"You don't have to do it alone," Rhiannon said, her voice filled with quiet reassurance. "But you must be prepared for what's to come. The Bloodborn are not just a name—they are a force, and that force is awakening."

Elara looked down at her hands, feeling the weight of the prophecy settle in her chest. She had always believed she was destined for greatness, but now she realized that destiny was not as simple as she had once thought. It would require more than strength, more than cunning. It would require the ultimate test of her resolve—and the willingness to sacrifice everything for the kingdom, for her people, and for the future of the Bloodborn.

As she stood there, contemplating the path that lay before her, Elara knew one thing for certain: the prophecy of the Bloodborn was not just a warning. It was a challenge. A challenge that would define her future, and the future of the kingdom itself.

Elara's thoughts whirled, her mind struggling to process the weight of the prophecy. She had always believed in her bloodline's strength, in the promise that the Bloodborn would be the ones to restore balance to the realm. But now, as the words of the seer echoed in her mind, doubt began to creep into her heart. Could she truly be the one to wield such power, or was she doomed to become the very instrument of destruction she had vowed to prevent?

The room around her felt stifling, the shadows deepening with every passing second. The prophecy was not just a tale from the past—it was a living, breathing entity, pressing against her every thought, every action. It was no longer just a matter of heritage or destiny. It was about survival.

"Elara," Rhiannon's voice broke through her thoughts again, softer this time. "You are not alone in this. You have allies, people who will fight beside you. But you must decide who can be trusted." Her eyes grew serious, her gaze intense as she met Elara's. "Not all of your bloodline will follow you. Some will see the prophecy as a chance to seize power for themselves. They will stop at nothing to claim what you have inherited. You must be prepared to confront them."

Elara swallowed hard. The notion of betrayal—of those who shared her blood turning against her—was more terrifying than any external threat. It was one thing to face an enemy in battle, but to face betrayal from within, from those closest to her, was an entirely different kind of war.

"I know what you're saying, Rhiannon," Elara said, her voice steady but tinged with fear. "But how can I know who to trust? How can I discern who is on my side when they all wear the same mask?"

Rhiannon gave a slight, knowing smile. "You don't need to look for masks, Elara. Look for the heart. The ones who truly care for the kingdom, for the people, will stand with you, no matter what. But the ones who seek power—who are blinded by ambition—will reveal themselves in time."

Elara nodded, though uncertainty still lingered in her chest. There was little time for second-guessing. The forces at play were vast, and if she didn't act soon, the prophecy would be fulfilled in ways she could not control. She would not let that happen. She couldn't.

With a deep breath, she turned to Rhiannon, determination hardening in her eyes. "Then we will find the allies we need. We will strengthen the kingdom, and we will face whatever the prophecy holds. But we will do it on our terms, not the terms of those who seek to twist our fate."

Rhiannon's gaze softened, a small nod of approval. "That's the spirit of a true Bloodborn, Elara. But remember—strength is not only found in power. Sometimes, it's found in sacrifice. In letting go of what you hold dear for the sake of the greater good."

Elara's heart tightened at the thought. Sacrifice. It had always seemed like a distant concept, something spoken of in legends and tales. But now, it felt more real than ever. She had known love, and she had known loss, but the true depth of sacrifice had yet to reveal itself to her. Would she be willing to lose everything—her family, her friends, her very soul—for the chance to save the kingdom?

"I will make whatever choice is necessary," Elara said, her voice firmer now, infused with the weight of her resolve. "But I will not allow our people to suffer at the hands of those who would destroy us."

Rhiannon placed a hand on her shoulder, her touch grounding. "Then we must prepare, Elara. The Bloodborn are not just your legacy—they are the legacy of a kingdom. And that legacy will either rise from the ashes, or be consumed by them."

Elara took a step back, her eyes narrowing with purpose. The path ahead would be fraught with danger, and the stakes had never been higher. But the prophecy had already set the stage. Now, it was up to her to play the part. To wield the power of the Bloodborn, to fight for her people, and to ensure that the legacy of her bloodline would not be the cause of their destruction.

The time to act had come.

2. The Betrayer's Whisper

○ Mistrust Among Allies

The tension in the grand hall was palpable. Elara stood at the head of the long, dark oak table, her crimson eyes scanning the gathered faces. The air carried the scent of burning wax and old parchment, but beneath it lay the stench of uncertainty. These were her allies—lords, warriors, and advisors—but she could feel the fractures forming between them like cracks in a glass about to shatter.

"You speak of unity," Lord Varian scoffed, arms crossed over his chest, his silver-streaked hair catching the flickering candlelight. "Yet we are no more than wolves waiting for the first sign of weakness." His voice was heavy with doubt, and Elara knew he wasn't alone in his skepticism.

Across from him, Rhiannon, the High Witch, drummed her fingers against the wood, her emerald nails glinting like poisoned daggers. "Varian is not wrong," she mused, her voice silk-soft but laced with steel. "Trust is a delicate thing, my Queen. And it has been shattered before."

Elara inhaled slowly, measuring her response. The past betrayals of the court still lingered like a fresh wound. Lord Garric, once her father's most loyal commander, had defected to the enemy. The Crimson Court had been infiltrated before—by spies, by whispers, by those who claimed loyalty but carried daggers behind their backs. Now, with the enemy pressing in and the kingdom teetering on the edge of war, the last thing she needed was doubt festering within her own ranks.

"You question my leadership?" she asked, her voice calm but edged with quiet warning.

Varian's jaw tightened. "I question the strength of this alliance. We are not bound by blood, Elara. We are bound by necessity. And necessity shifts like the tide."

A murmur rippled through the room. She could see it in their eyes—some shared his fear. Some were waiting for someone else to make the first move.

"I have no time for doubt," she said, stepping forward. "Nor for disloyalty."

Lord Dain, a battle-scarred warrior with a face like chiseled stone, leaned forward. "Then prove to us, Queen of the Bloodborn, that this kingdom is worth bleeding for."

The challenge hung between them. It was not just a call for words, but for action.

Elara's fingers curled into fists at her sides. She would not let doubt unravel what she had fought to build. If they needed proof of her strength, she would give them something they could not deny.

"Then listen well," she said, her voice carrying the weight of steel and fire. "Before the next moon rises, I will lead the charge myself. And I will bring you the head of our greatest enemy."

Silence. Then, one by one, heads bowed in reluctant agreement.

Mistrust still lingered in the room like an unspoken curse, but now, it had been met with something stronger. A promise.

And Elara never broke a promise.

The silence in the hall stretched, heavy with unspoken thoughts. Elara held their gazes, refusing to waver. Doubt had taken root among her allies, but she would not let it grow into something uncontrollable. If trust could not be restored through words alone, then she would carve it into existence with blood and steel.

Varian was the first to break the silence, his expression unreadable. "If you lead the charge yourself, you risk everything," he said slowly. "A queen is not meant to stand on the front lines."

Elara tilted her head slightly, amusement flickering in her crimson eyes. "A queen is meant to lead, Lord Varian. If that means standing where the battle is fiercest, then so be it."

Across the table, Rhiannon leaned back in her chair, a sly smile playing at her lips. "Your courage is admirable," she murmured, though there was something unreadable in her gaze. "But tell me, my Queen—who do you trust to stand beside you when the blades are drawn?"

That was the question, wasn't it?

Elara's gaze swept over the gathered faces. Warriors and nobles, commanders and spies—each had pledged loyalty to her cause, but loyalty was a fragile thing, easily bent by fear or ambition. She could not afford another betrayal.

She turned to Dain, the grizzled warrior who had fought by her father's side long before she had claimed the throne. "You will command the vanguard."

The old warrior nodded, his face a mask of hardened resolve. "It will be done."

Her gaze shifted to Rhiannon. "And you will ensure that our enemies do not see what is coming before it is too late."

The High Witch's smile deepened, and she inclined her head. "As you command."

Finally, her eyes locked onto Varian. "And you, Lord Varian?" she asked, her voice steady. "Will you stand with me, or will you continue to doubt?"

Varian's jaw tightened. For a moment, she thought he might refuse, that his mistrust had already poisoned him beyond repair. But then, after a long pause, he nodded.

"I will stand with you," he said. "For now."

It was not the unwavering loyalty she desired, but it was a start.

Elara turned back to the room, her expression unreadable. "Then prepare yourselves," she commanded. "We ride at dawn."

As the gathering began to disperse, she felt the weight of unseen eyes upon her. Even now, even among those who had sworn fealty, she knew the shadows still whispered.

Mistrust had not been vanquished.

It had merely been postponed.

○ Shadows of the Past

The cold wind howled through the narrow corridors of the abandoned keep, carrying whispers of a past that refused to die. Elara moved silently through the ruins, her crimson cloak billowing behind her like a specter of forgotten wars. The scent of damp stone and decayed wood clung to the air, mixing with the distant aroma of burning torches from the city below. This place had once been a stronghold of the Bloodborn, a sanctuary where kings and queens had conspired, where betrayals had been sealed with blood. Now, it was nothing but a graveyard of lost ambitions.

She ran her fingers along the cracked walls, feeling the echoes of memories long buried. The past had not been kind to this kingdom, nor to those who had ruled it. Here, in the remnants of what once was, she could almost hear the voices of those who had come before her—their warnings, their regrets.

"Elara."

The voice was soft yet edged with familiarity. She turned to find Rhiannon standing at the entrance, her dark eyes filled with something unreadable. There was always an unease between them, a tension born of secrets neither was willing to speak aloud.

"You shouldn't be here," Rhiannon said, stepping forward, her boots echoing against the stone.

Elara let out a slow breath. "Neither should you."

Silence stretched between them like a fragile thread, one that could snap at the slightest touch. They both knew why they were here. The past had drawn them back, forcing them to confront what had been left unfinished.

Rhiannon's gaze swept over the ruins. "Do you remember what happened in this hall?"

Elara's jaw tightened. "I remember everything."

She had been a child when she last stood in this place, hiding behind a pillar as her father, King Vaelin, had condemned his own brother to death. The echoes of steel against stone, the scent of spilled blood, the cries of betrayal—it had all been carved into her memory like an open wound. That was the day she learned that loyalty was an illusion, and that power came at a cost.

Rhiannon studied her, as if trying to decipher whether she was the same girl who had once trembled in the shadows. "The past doesn't rest, Elara. And neither do those who were wronged."

Elara met her gaze, her expression unreadable. "Then perhaps it's time to finish what was started."

Thunder rumbled in the distance, as if the heavens themselves had heard her vow.

Rhiannon studied Elara for a long moment, her expression unreadable, but there was something in her eyes—something cautious, as if she were measuring the weight of those words. Then, with a slow exhale, she turned away, stepping deeper into the ruins.

"If you truly believe that," Rhiannon murmured, her fingers brushing against a broken stone pillar, "then you must be prepared for what finishing it will cost you."

Elara followed her, her boots crunching against loose debris. The past had already cost her more than she cared to acknowledge—her childhood, her trust, her belief in anything other than the cold reality of power. And yet, standing here, with the scent of old blood still lingering in the cracks of the stone, she realized that she had never really left this place.

"What do you know?" she asked, her voice steady.

Rhiannon glanced at her over her shoulder. "More than you'd like me to."

Elara clenched her jaw. "Then say it."

Rhiannon hesitated, then sighed. "The king's death wasn't the end of the war—it was the beginning of something else. Something older than the Bloodborn. You think you're fighting for a throne, Elara, but you're fighting against ghosts far older than this kingdom."

Elara's brow furrowed. "And what would you call them?"

Rhiannon tilted her head, the flickering torchlight casting sharp shadows across her face. "Monsters. The kind that don't die."

A chill that had nothing to do with the wind crept down Elara's spine. She wanted to dismiss Rhiannon's words as riddles, but deep down, she knew better. The Bloodborn had always been more than just a royal bloodline—they were bound to something greater, something darker.

Elara exhaled slowly, steadying her thoughts. "Then let them come."

Rhiannon shook her head, a sad smile ghosting her lips. "They already have."

A sound echoed through the ruined hall—soft at first, like the shifting of stone, then unmistakably human. A whisper. A breath. A presence.

Elara's hand went to the dagger at her hip as she turned sharply, scanning the darkness beyond the crumbling pillars. The ruins had always been abandoned, but now, the air felt different—charged, alive, waiting.

Then she saw it.

A shadow moved against the far wall, too fluid, too deliberate to be the wind. A figure in the dark, watching.

"Elara," Rhiannon murmured, her voice barely above a whisper. "We're not alone."

○ The First Strike

The night air was thick with the scent of damp earth and blood. Elara stood atop the crumbling watchtower, her crimson cloak billowing behind her like the wings of a specter. Below, the torches of her advancing forces flickered in the distance, their steady march toward the enemy stronghold a silent promise of reckoning.

The scouts had returned only moments ago, their reports confirming what she already suspected—Vanguard's forces were massing beyond the Black Hollow, preparing for a preemptive assault. But she would not give them the chance. She would strike first.

A figure moved beside her. Commander Kael, his battle-worn armor catching the moonlight, studied the valley below with narrowed eyes. "They're not expecting an attack tonight," he said. "Their defenses are still shifting, their supply lines exposed."

Elara nodded, fingers tightening around the hilt of her blade. "Then we make them bleed before they even raise their swords."

The strategy had been decided hours ago. Her warriors, hardened by years of conflict, had already begun to position themselves along the ridges and in the dense forest that bordered the enemy encampment. Silent and unseen, they would strike like phantoms in the dark.

A single raven cawed in the distance. The signal.

Kael turned to her, awaiting the command.

"Go," Elara said.

Within moments, shadows spilled from the treeline. Arrows cut through the stillness, striking their targets with deadly precision. The enemy's first cries of alarm were drowned by the clash of steel as Elara's forces stormed the camp.

She moved with them, her blade a streak of silver in the moonlight. The first soldier that turned toward her barely had time to raise his weapon before she drove her sword through his ribs. He crumpled, and she stepped over him, eyes already scanning for the next threat.

Chaos erupted. The Vanguard troops scrambled to mount a defense, but they had been caught off guard. Tents collapsed, flames spread, and bodies fell beneath the relentless assault.

A roar split the air. A hulking warrior charged at Elara, an axe raised high. She sidestepped his swing, feeling the wind of the strike brush past her face before she drove her dagger into his throat. He fell without a sound.

Kael fought beside her, his movements precise, efficient. They had done this dance a hundred times before, side by side in battle, always pressing forward, always fighting toward victory.

But something was wrong.

Through the chaos, she spotted movement beyond the ridge. A second wave of troops. More than she had anticipated.

Damn it.

A trap.

The realization hit her like a fist to the chest. They had underestimated Vanguard.

"Elara!" Kael's voice was sharp, urgent. "We need to regroup!"

She hesitated, unwilling to concede ground. But the battlefield was shifting. If they didn't act now, they would be the ones caught between the hammer and the anvil.

With a fierce growl, she raised her sword high. "Fall back to the ridge! Regroup and hold the line!"

Her warriors obeyed without question, retreating in practiced formation. As they withdrew, Vanguard's reinforcements surged forward, their battle cries tearing through the night.

Elara's heart pounded. This was only the beginning.

The first strike had been hers—but the war was far from over.

The retreat was calculated, precise—every warrior moving with discipline honed by years of war. Elara led the charge up the ridge, her crimson cloak flashing like a beacon amidst the shifting tide of battle. Arrows rained down as Vanguard's reinforcements pursued, but her soldiers knew this terrain. They had chosen it for a reason.

Kael reached her side, his breath ragged but his grip steady on his twin blades. "We can't hold them off for long if they push harder. We need a countermeasure."

Elara's eyes flickered toward the ridge's peak. The trap Vanguard had set for them was clever, but they weren't the only ones who had planned for contingencies.

She lifted two fingers in a silent command. From the shadows above, her archers unleashed hell.

A hail of arrows darkened the sky, striking down the first wave of advancing soldiers. Screams of agony filled the air as bodies collapsed, some tumbling back into their own ranks, disrupting Vanguard's momentum.

But it wasn't enough. More soldiers poured in, their armor glinting in the moonlight, their war cries rising like thunder.

A deep horn blast cut through the chaos—a signal from the western flank. Reinforcements.

Elara's pulse quickened.

Through the trees, a second force emerged—her allies, led by General Soren, a towering figure clad in blackened steel. He wasted no time. His warriors crashed into Vanguard's ranks like a battering ram, forcing them into a chaotic scramble.

For the first time that night, the battle shifted in her favor.

Elara seized the moment, charging forward with Kael at her side. Their blades cut through the fray, the scent of blood thick in the cold night air. She ducked beneath an enemy's swing, her dagger finding the soft space between his armor plates. A second attacker lunged, but she twisted, driving her sword through his gut.

Vanguard's soldiers faltered under the combined assault. What had begun as an ambush against her had turned into a slaughter against them.

But victory was never without its price.

From the corner of her vision, she saw one of her men fall—a blade buried in his back. Then another.

And then—

A sharp pain erupted in her side.

Elara staggered, her fingers instinctively pressing against the wound. Warm blood seeped through her armor.

Kael's roar cut through the noise. He was beside her in an instant, his blade flashing as he cut down the attacker who had struck her.

"Elara!" His voice was strained, desperate.

She gritted her teeth, pushing past the searing pain. She had suffered worse. She would not fall. Not now.

"Keep pushing forward!" she commanded, voice steel despite the wound. "Break their lines!"

Kael hesitated for only a second before nodding. He turned back to the battlefield, his movements swift and deadly, rallying their forces.

The battle raged on, but now, Vanguard was breaking. Some fled into the trees, others fought to the death. By the time the dust settled, the ground was littered with bodies, the silence of the dead heavier than the echoes of war.

Elara pressed a hand against her injury, breathing hard as she surveyed the aftermath. Soren approached, wiping blood from his blade.

"A hard-won victory," he said, voice low. "But a victory nonetheless."

She exhaled, nodding. "For now."

Because she knew this was only the beginning.

The first strike had been theirs—but Vanguard would not let this go unanswered.

3. The Crimson Court

○ A Gathering of the Royals

The grand hall of Blackthorn Keep was bathed in the cold glow of moonlight streaming through the tall stained-glass windows. Shadows stretched long across the polished obsidian floor, where the sigil of the Bloodborn Queen gleamed—a crimson serpent coiled around a silver crown. The air was thick with unspoken tension as nobles and rulers from the farthest reaches of the realm gathered under one roof, their whispered conversations weaving a web of alliances and betrayals.

Elara stood at the head of the great table, clad in deep red silk, her dark eyes scanning the assembled lords and ladies with measured intensity. Power clung to her like a second skin, the weight of her crown pressing against her temples as she held herself with the effortless grace of a ruler who had fought too hard to be questioned. She knew why they had come—not out of loyalty, but out of fear.

King Roderic of the Ironclad Dominion was the first to speak, his voice rough from years spent in battle. "This war cannot be won alone, Queen Elara. We have fought our own skirmishes against the rogue factions, but the tide is turning. Your enemies do not respect borders. They do not play by the rules of kings and queens."

A murmur of agreement rippled through the hall. Beside Roderic, Queen Lysandra of the Verdant Isles, draped in emerald and pearls, leaned forward, her sharp eyes gleaming with calculation. "The rogue clans are growing bolder. My spies report that Vanguard is amassing forces in the north. We may each rule our own kingdoms, but a storm does not choose its victims."

Elara remained silent, letting the words settle, letting them feel the weight of their own vulnerability. She had learned long ago that silence was a weapon just as powerful as any sword. When she finally spoke, her voice cut through the murmurs like a blade.

"I did not summon you here to remind you of our shared enemy," she said, her tone smooth but unyielding. "I summoned you to decide whether you will stand beside me or be trampled beneath the coming war."

Across the table, Duke Valen of the Ashen Coast exhaled sharply, his fingers tightening around the silver goblet in his hand. "And if we refuse?"

Elara's lips curled into the hint of a smile, though there was no warmth in it. "Then you will have sealed your fate. There will be no neutrality when the war begins. The Bloodborn do not forget, nor do we forgive."

Silence fell once more, heavier than before. Some shifted uncomfortably in their seats; others exchanged wary glances. They had come expecting negotiations, expecting leverage. Instead, they had found a queen who had already decided their fates.

A slow clap echoed through the hall, drawing all eyes to the far end of the room. Leaning against a marble pillar, his golden eyes gleaming with amusement, was Dorian Vex, the rogue prince of the Eastern Expanse. He pushed off the pillar with casual ease, striding toward the table as though he belonged there.

"You always did have a flair for the dramatic, Elara," he mused, his voice a lazy drawl. "But let's not pretend this is a choice. You don't need allies—you need soldiers. And some of us," he gestured toward the gathered royals, "aren't inclined to die for a queen whose throne is still drenched in fresh blood."

The room tensed, but Elara only tilted her head slightly. "Then perhaps you should choose your next words carefully, Prince Dorian. Because in this room, you are surrounded by those who know that the only thing more dangerous than war... is defying a queen with nothing left to lose."

Dorian held her gaze for a long moment before finally chuckling, raising his hands in mock surrender. "Very well. Consider me... intrigued."

One by one, the rulers nodded, some reluctantly, some with quiet resolve. The decision had been made.

The gathering of royals had begun as a test of power. Now, it was a pact forged in blood.

And the war was only beginning.

The tension in the room did not dissipate, even as the gathered rulers came to the grim understanding that their fates were now entwined with Elara's. It was not a matter of loyalty, nor was it even a matter of survival—this was a game of power, and none of them were willing to fold so easily.

Elara let the silence stretch for another breath before she turned, signaling to the attendants who had been waiting in the shadows. At her command, the heavy iron doors swung open, revealing a line of soldiers clad in black and crimson, their armor polished to a deadly sheen. They carried trays—not of food, but of parchment, wax seals, and daggers.

"You will sign the Blood Pact," Elara declared, stepping aside as the attendants placed the documents before each ruler. "A binding contract between our kingdoms. We move as one, fight as one, and should any of us betray the alliance..." Her gaze swept over them, lingering on those she knew were the most reluctant. "The consequences will be... absolute."

The nobles exchanged wary glances. The Blood Pact was no ordinary treaty. It was an oath written in blood, bound by magic older than the kingdoms themselves. To break it was to invite ruin—not just for the traitor, but for their entire bloodline.

King Roderic, ever the pragmatist, was the first to act. Without hesitation, he took the dagger provided, drew it across his palm, and pressed his bleeding hand against the parchment. The ink absorbed the blood, glowing faintly before sealing itself with his sigil. He sat back, jaw tight, but his decision was made.

Queen Lysandra followed, though with considerably more reluctance. "You leave us little choice, Elara," she murmured as she let a single drop of her blood fall onto the parchment.

Duke Valen hesitated, fingers gripping the dagger tightly. "And if this alliance fails?" he asked, his voice measured. "If we are overrun, if we fall before our enemies—what then?"

Elara stepped closer, her presence a shadow looming over him. "Then we die knowing we did not cower. But make no mistake, Valen. We will not fall."

One by one, the rulers sealed their oaths, some with grim determination, others with veiled resentment. When it was Dorian's turn, he took his time, twirling the dagger between his fingers before finally pressing the tip against his palm.

"Very well, my queen," he drawled, letting the blood drip onto the parchment. "I suppose this is how we begin our descent into madness."

Elara met his gaze, her expression unreadable. "No, Dorian," she said softly. "This is how we reclaim what is ours."

With the pact sealed, the air in the hall grew heavier, as if the walls themselves bore witness to the agreement that had been made. The gathering of royals had come to an end—but what they had set in motion would shape the future of the realm.

Elara turned toward the towering map that loomed over the great table, her gloved fingers tracing the borders of her kingdom. War was no longer a looming threat.

It had already begun.

○ The Hidden Agenda

A heavy silence settled over the Crimson Court as Elara observed the gathered nobles, their expressions veiled behind polite smiles and half-lowered eyes. The grand hall was bathed in the dim glow of chandeliers, the golden light flickering over the velvet drapes and polished marble floor. Conversations hummed in soft murmurs, but Elara could sense the weight of unspoken words pressing against the air.

She was no stranger to deception. Every whispered alliance, every subtle glance exchanged across the room carried the scent of hidden motives. The council of elders had called this gathering under the guise of unity, but Elara knew better—this was a test, a quiet war waged with diplomacy rather than swords.

Standing at the edge of the chamber, she kept her expression unreadable as she watched Lord Castien lean toward Lady Veyra, his fingers barely grazing the rim of his goblet as he spoke. Her reaction was slight—a tilt of her head, a fleeting smirk—but it was enough to tell Elara that they were scheming.

The weight of her crown felt heavier tonight.

"You should be careful where you set your gaze," a low voice murmured beside her.

Elara did not flinch as Rhiannon, the witch who had saved her life more than once, stepped into the shadows beside her. Draped in black, her dark curls cascaded over her shoulders, framing her sharp, knowing eyes.

"They plot," Elara said, voice barely above a whisper.

"They always have," Rhiannon replied, studying the room with the eyes of a predator. "But tonight, there is something different. I can feel it."

Elara turned slightly. "What do you mean?"

Rhiannon's fingers brushed against the silver ring on her hand, the faint glow of her magic barely perceptible to those untrained in the art.

"There is an energy in the air, something woven beneath the surface. Magic, but laced with deceit. Someone is setting the stage for betrayal."

A slow, creeping sensation curled down Elara's spine. She scanned the room again, her mind sifting through possibilities. Who among them was bold enough to move against her?

Before she could voice her thoughts, a servant approached, bowing deeply before extending a small parchment sealed with the insignia of House Eldrin.

"A message, Your Majesty," he said, eyes averted.

Elara took the letter, breaking the seal with precise fingers. The words within were simple, yet chilling in their implications:

Trust no one. The dagger is already drawn.

Her grip tightened around the parchment, but she did not allow her mask to falter. With a slow breath, she folded the note, slipping it beneath her sleeve.

If betrayal was in motion, she would be ready.

Elara felt the weight of the warning settle deep in her chest, but she schooled her features into an expression of calm detachment. The dance of deception was not new to her—she had waded through shadows long before claiming the throne, and she had no intention of falling victim to unseen daggers now.

She turned to Rhiannon, her voice low. "If there is magic at play, I need to know who wields it."

Rhiannon studied her carefully before giving a slight nod. "I will find the source." With a whisper of incantation, she vanished into the crowd, her presence melting into the dimly lit chamber as though she had never stood there at all.

Elara took a slow step forward, forcing herself to mingle, to appear unaware of the silent war unfolding around her. The nobles were watching—always watching. She could feel their gazes like the brush of phantom fingers along her spine.

Lord Castien met her eyes across the hall and raised his goblet slightly in a silent salute. A calculated move. His alliances had always been fluid, his loyalties shifting like the tide. But now, there was something different about the way he studied her, a hint of amusement, of knowledge he should not have possessed.

The warning in the letter rang in her mind like a death knell.

The dagger is already drawn.

Elara moved toward him, her steps slow and deliberate. If he knew something, she would pull it from him—one way or another.

"Your Majesty," Castien greeted smoothly as she reached his side, his voice touched with the familiar arrogance of someone who had spent a lifetime playing this game. "A rare pleasure."

Elara allowed herself a small, enigmatic smile. "I thought it time we spoke, Lord Castien. It has been too long."

"Indeed." His eyes flickered with interest, but he was careful. "One can only hope our conversation will be more enlightening than the ones filling this hall tonight."

She tilted her head slightly. "A strange choice of words."

Castien chuckled, swirling the wine in his goblet. "Is it?"

Before she could press further, a sudden hush fell over the chamber. The grand doors at the far end of the hall groaned open, and a cloaked figure stepped inside.

The shift in the air was immediate. Tension rippled through the room, quiet gasps and hushed murmurs spreading like wildfire.

Elara's blood ran cold.

The figure lowered their hood, revealing a face she had not seen in years.

Prince Kael.

The man who should have been dead.

○ Power Struggles

The air in the royal court was thick with tension, a storm brewing not just outside the walls of the palace but within its very heart. Elara stood at the grand window, gazing out over the city that stretched beneath her, a kingdom on the verge of change. Her kingdom. But how much longer would she be allowed to rule it?

She had once been certain of her place, the undisputed queen with the blood of the ancient kings coursing through her veins. But now, as whispers of rebellion and discontent spread like wildfire, doubt gnawed at her resolve. In the distance, she could see the banners of her enemies rising, their darkened silhouettes flapping in the wind. They were ready to strike.

The throne, once a symbol of her power, had become a seat of vulnerability. Elara knew that the struggle for power wasn't just a matter of armies clashing on the battlefield. It was much more insidious than that. In the courtyards and hallways of the palace, in the shadowed chambers where secrets were whispered, alliances were shifting, loyalties were fractured, and hidden agendas festered like wounds waiting to open.

At her side, Lord Galen, her most trusted advisor, spoke in hushed tones. His face, usually calm and composed, now betrayed a rare hint of anxiety. "My Queen, you cannot ignore it any longer. The nobles are beginning to see you as weak. They question your authority, your judgment. There are talks of replacing you—"

Elara turned sharply, her piercing gaze locking with his. She had always trusted Galen, but this felt different. His words, though meant to warn, felt like a betrayal. She could see the shadows of doubt flicker in his eyes, and the realization hit her like a cold wave. Even the ones she had relied on the most were beginning to entertain thoughts of her downfall.

"You think they could replace me?" Her voice was low, dangerous. "After everything I've done for this kingdom?"

Galen hesitated, but only for a moment. "I think they believe your time is over. The bloodline you carry may be ancient, but it has become a symbol of stagnation, not strength."

Her fingers tightened around the hilt of the dagger hidden at her waist, a subtle gesture, but one that spoke volumes. Elara was no stranger to power struggles. She had been raised in a world where betrayal was as common as breath, where loyalty could be bought with a glance and discarded with a coin. She knew that power, once gained, was never truly hers to keep. It was always fleeting, always fragile.

Outside, the wind howled, a harbinger of the storm to come. Elara's mind raced, weighing her options, but she could not afford to hesitate. If she did, the kingdom she had fought so hard to build would slip through her fingers like sand.

She turned back to the window, her face a mask of resolve. "Then I will remind them of what happens when they challenge me." Her words were sharp, decisive. "Let them come."

Galen stepped back, his brow furrowed, but he knew better than to argue now. Elara had made her decision. The game of power had shifted, and she would play it with every weapon at her disposal—no matter the cost.

In the coming days, the struggle for the throne would escalate. The whispers would grow louder, the alliances more dangerous. The nobles who had once been her allies would now become her fiercest adversaries. And as the winds of change swept through the palace, Elara knew she would either emerge victorious—or be swallowed by the shadows of those who sought to tear her down.

In the end, there could be only one ruler. One victor. And it would be Elara who decided who that would be.

The days that followed were filled with unrest. Rumors of Elara's perceived weakness swirled like smoke, growing thicker with each passing hour. The nobles, once loyal to her cause, began to edge away, seeking to align themselves with whoever they believed would hold the true power. The council meetings, which had once been filled with discussions of prosperity and defense, now became battlegrounds of verbal duels, each word laden with unspoken threats and veiled ambitions.

Elara moved through her court like a predator, aware of every glance, every hushed conversation. Her gaze lingered on the faces of the lords and ladies who surrounded her, each one a potential enemy hiding in plain sight. Trust had become a commodity she could no longer afford.

In the grand hall, as the nobles gathered for a meeting that was to determine the future of the realm, Elara could feel the weight of their gazes on her. The tension was palpable, thick enough to suffocate the air. She stood at the head of the room, her regal presence a stark contrast to the nervous energy of her court.

Lord Tiberius, once a loyal ally, now stood at the forefront of the dissenters. His tall frame, usually a beacon of strength, now seemed to loom like a shadow over the room. His eyes, cold and calculating, locked with Elara's.

"It seems the time has come to discuss the future of our kingdom," he began, his voice smooth, yet carrying an edge of defiance. "Our queen, once the pride of the realm, now stands at the precipice of ruin. The people no longer believe in her strength. They believe she is lost to them."

Elara's heart raced, but her expression remained unreadable. She had known this moment would come. The council had become a snake pit, each member vying for a place at the head of the feast. She took a step forward, her voice cutting through the tension like a blade.

"Do they believe I am lost?" she asked, her tone unwavering. "I think not, Lord Tiberius. They fear me. They fear the power I hold, the power that is mine by right."

The room fell silent. The nobles exchanged wary glances, unsure of how to respond to her bold assertion.

"But even fear can fade," Tiberius continued, a smirk playing at the corners of his lips. "And a throne built on fear is one that is easily toppled."

"I do not rule with fear alone, Tiberius," Elara shot back, her voice rising, powerful. "I rule with strength, with conviction. And when the time comes, I will show you just how strong I am."

Her words were not just a declaration of intent but a challenge. She could see the flicker of doubt in Tiberius's eyes, but he quickly masked it. The other nobles shifted uncomfortably, unsure whether they should rally behind her or seek their own advantage.

In that moment, Elara knew she had to act swiftly, decisively. The power struggle had become a game of survival. She could no longer wait for her enemies to make their move. The time for subtlety had passed.

Later that night, Elara summoned her most trusted generals to the war room. Among them was Captain Rafe, a hardened soldier who had fought beside her for years. His loyalty was unquestionable, but even he had begun to question the strength of her reign.

"What's the plan, my queen?" Rafe asked, his voice steady but filled with concern.

"We take control," Elara said, her eyes flashing with a cold determination. "We strike at their hearts, their very sense of security. We remind them who rules this kingdom. And we do it before they have the chance to strike at me first."

Rafe nodded, his expression serious. "You mean to move against the nobles directly?"

"No," Elara replied. "Not directly. We'll let them think they've won for now. We'll stir chaos, create confusion, and when they least expect it, we'll strike."

Her plan was risky, but Elara knew that the only way to regain control was to force her enemies into a corner. They had grown complacent, believing they had the upper hand. Now, it was time to shatter their illusions.

The next few days were filled with covert actions. Elara's agents infiltrated the noble houses, sowing discord and mistrust. Rumors of betrayal, secret meetings, and hidden alliances spread like wildfire, causing chaos within the factions. The nobles began to turn on one another, each afraid of being exposed as a traitor.

As the tension reached its peak, Elara prepared for her final move. She had spent years building her influence in the shadows, creating a network of spies, mercenaries, and loyalists who could be relied upon when the time was right. Now, that time had come.

The night before the council meeting, Elara stood alone in the throne room, staring at the empty seat that had once been a symbol of her unquestioned authority. The throne seemed to mock her, its grandeur now a reminder of how precarious her position had become. But Elara refused to be intimidated. She had come too far to falter now.

When the council met the next day, it would be different. The room would be filled with the weight of her power, and the nobles would understand that challenging her reign was no longer an option.

The game had changed. And Elara was ready to play.

4. A Legacy of Blood

○ Elara's Burden

Elara stood alone in the dimly lit chamber, the weight of the crown pressing down on her as though it were an anchor dragging her deeper into the darkness. The walls around her, once adorned with the grandeur of her ancestors, now seemed to close in, suffocating her with their cold, unyielding stone. Her fingers brushed lightly over the intricate carvings of the throne's backrest, tracing the ancient symbols that had been passed down through generations, each one a reminder of the bloodline she was born into — a bloodline cursed, revered, and feared by all.

For years, Elara had embraced her destiny, the prophecy that declared her the rightful heir to the throne. She had believed in the righteousness of her cause, the belief that her blood would be the salvation of the kingdom. But now, as she gazed into the mirror that hung on the far wall, she saw nothing but the reflection of a woman trapped in a web of her own making. The kingdom, once vibrant and full of hope, now teetered on the brink of collapse, and she was helpless to stop it.

The weight of her ancestors' sins hung heavy on her shoulders. The blood that ran through her veins was not just a gift, but a curse — one that bound her to the throne and to the kingdom's fate. Her bloodline had been marked by power, by bloodshed, and by a hunger for control that had lasted for centuries. Every decision she made, every action she took, was stained with the legacy of her forebears.

She had often wondered if it was possible to escape this fate, to walk away from the throne and the endless demands of leadership. But the answer was always the same — no. The moment she was born, she had been destined for this life, this burden. Her parents, who had both been victims of the kingdom's brutal politics, had groomed her for this role from the very beginning. They had taught her how to rule, how to command, how to be unyielding in the face of opposition. But they had never prepared her for the cost.

The court was a sea of wolves, each one circling, waiting for the moment when her resolve would falter, when her power would weaken. And yet, it wasn't just the external threats that tormented Elara. It was the whispers in her own mind, the questions that never ceased. Was she truly capable of leading? Was she worthy of this crown? Could she bear the weight of her bloodline's sins, or would she become another victim of their destructive legacy?

Her thoughts were interrupted by the faintest sound — a soft knock at the door. Elara quickly straightened, wiping the unease from her face. "Enter," she called, her voice steady, though the storm within her raged on.

The door creaked open, and a figure stepped inside — Rhiannon, her most trusted advisor. The older woman's sharp eyes scanned the room, lingering on Elara for a moment before she spoke. "Your Majesty," she began, her tone respectful yet carrying an undercurrent of concern, "there are matters that require your immediate attention. The council awaits your presence."

Elara nodded, though her mind remained distant. She had always admired Rhiannon's unwavering loyalty, her wisdom, but today, even the comfort of her advisor's presence could not quell the rising tide of doubt in her chest. As she turned to leave the chamber, Elara cast one final glance at her reflection, the burden of her legacy weighing heavier than ever.

The road ahead was fraught with peril. Her bloodline's dark secrets were beginning to surface, threatening to undo everything she had fought to protect. She would have to confront the demons of her past — the choices made by those before her — and ultimately decide if she could rewrite the future of her kingdom, or if she was doomed to repeat the mistakes of the past.

And so, with each step she took toward the council, Elara understood that her burden was not just the crown upon her head. It was the heavy weight of history, of destiny, and of the power that had been passed down to her, waiting for her to either embrace it or shatter under its force.

But for now, there was no turning back.

As Elara walked down the long corridor, the rhythmic echo of her footsteps seemed to stretch the silence, a stark reminder of the isolation that had come with her position. The grand stone hallways of the palace, with their high vaulted ceilings and towering arches, felt more like a labyrinth than a home. Despite the opulence of her surroundings, there was no warmth here, only cold stone and ancient whispers. The walls, lined with portraits of past monarchs, seemed to judge her with every step, their eyes filled with expectations she could never fully meet.

Rhiannon walked silently beside her, always close but never intrusive. The older woman had been a constant presence in Elara's life, a guiding hand during her most trying times. She had been there when Elara's parents had fallen, when the kingdom had fractured into warring factions, and when Elara had been forced to ascend the throne much sooner than anyone had anticipated. Rhiannon had been more than an advisor; she had been a second mother, always ready to provide counsel, to offer solace when Elara felt the world closing in.

But today, even Rhiannon's comforting presence could not ease the storm brewing within Elara. Her mind raced with questions and fears, each one more paralyzing than the last. How long could she keep the peace? How long could she hold onto the power she so desperately needed to protect her people? The council that awaited her was not just a gathering of advisors; it was a reminder that the fate of the kingdom rested squarely on her shoulders. And in that moment, it felt like a weight she could no longer bear alone.

As they entered the council chamber, Elara felt the familiar tension in the air. The long, polished table was surrounded by the kingdom's most influential figures — nobles, generals, and diplomats — all seated with expressions of expectancy, waiting for their queen to take her place. At the far end of the table, Lord Darian, the kingdom's most powerful general, sat with his steely gaze fixed firmly on her. His reputation for ruthlessness was well-known, and though he respected Elara's authority, there was an undercurrent of doubt in his eyes that she had come to dread.

"Your Majesty," he said, rising as she entered, his voice commanding but respectful. "The situation grows dire. The neighboring kingdoms stir with unrest, and the people grow restless. We need to act, and we need to act now."

Elara took her seat at the head of the table, feeling the weight of every gaze upon her. "And what would you suggest, General?" she asked, her voice steady despite the growing unease in her chest.

Lord Darian's expression hardened as he leaned forward, his hands clasped tightly together. "We must strike before they have a chance to strike us. Our borders are vulnerable, and the longer we wait, the more likely it is that we will be caught off guard. The time for diplomacy has passed."

Elara's fingers clenched around the armrests of her chair, her heart pounding in her chest. It wasn't the first time Darian had suggested such a course of action, but something in his tone today felt different. There was an urgency to his words, a quiet desperation that she had not seen before. She glanced at Rhiannon, who gave a subtle shake of her head, a silent warning not to be swayed by Darian's pressure.

"We cannot rush into war without careful consideration," Elara said, her voice firm. "The consequences could be disastrous. We need to find a way to calm the unrest without resorting to bloodshed."

The room fell silent, the council members exchanging uncertain glances. Darian's jaw tightened, but he did not press the matter further. Instead, another voice spoke up from the far side of the room — Lady Isolde, one of the kingdom's foremost diplomats, known for her sharp wit and even sharper tongue.

"Perhaps it is not war that we need to fear, but the fractures within our own walls," she said, her voice cool and measured. "The nobles are divided, Your Majesty. There are those who still question your rule, who doubt your ability to lead. The longer we delay action, the more likely it is that they will find an opportunity to undermine you."

Elara's gaze flicked to Isolde, noting the cold calculation in her eyes. The diplomat was always keen to find a way to manipulate the kingdom's power dynamics, but there was truth in her words. Her bloodline was one of the oldest in the kingdom, and many of the nobles still viewed Elara's ascension with suspicion. Her parents' death had created a power vacuum, and while Elara had been crowned queen, there were whispers of rebellion in the shadows, whispers that threatened to tear the kingdom apart.

"We will address the noble dissenters," Elara said, her voice low but resolute. "But I will not let the kingdom fall to infighting. I will not let us destroy ourselves from within."

She could feel the weight of her words settling over the room, and for a brief moment, the tension seemed to lift. But it wasn't enough to quell the storm that raged inside her. She was caught between the desire to prove herself — to show that she was worthy of her crown — and the knowledge that every decision she made would bring her closer to the breaking point.

As the council continued, Elara found herself retreating into her own thoughts. Each word, each suggestion, each proposal felt like another piece of the burden she had to bear. She was their queen, their savior, their hope. But in that moment, she felt more like a prisoner, shackled by the very thing she had been born to inherit.

And the worst part? She knew that no matter how hard she fought, no matter how many battles she won, there would always be more. The crown was not just a symbol of power; it was a constant reminder of everything she had to lose.

The meeting continued, but Elara's mind drifted. She had a decision to make — one that would shape the future of her kingdom, and perhaps even her own soul. And she could only hope that, in the end, she would find a way to bear the burden of her bloodline without losing herself entirely.

○ The Curse of the Ancients

Elara stood on the balcony of the castle, her gaze lost in the vast expanse of the darkened horizon. The moon hung high, its pale light casting long shadows over the kingdom she once knew so well. Now, everything felt different — fractured, like a shattered mirror reflecting a distorted version of reality. Her heart ached, a constant reminder of the weight she carried, not just as a queen but as the last descendant of the Bloodborn.

Her bloodline, once revered and feared, now lay on the brink of extinction. The curse of the ancients was not just a legend, a tale spun by the elders to frighten children. No, it was real. And it was hunting her.

The whispers had begun years ago, when her father, King Aldric, first fell ill. At the time, they had seemed nothing more than rumors, the kind that circulated among the court when uncertainty loomed. But as the years passed, and as the symptoms grew more pronounced — the feverish rages, the paranoia, the strange visions — Elara had come to understand the truth. Her father had been marked by the curse, a curse that had plagued their bloodline for centuries.

She had hoped, foolishly, that the curse would skip her, that the gods might show mercy on her. But the signs were unmistakable. Her own dreams had become twisted with visions of an ancient temple buried beneath the earth, of dark figures chanting in a language older than time itself. In those dreams, she saw her ancestors, their faces twisted in agony, as they tried to pass on a warning. A warning she couldn't fully understand — not yet.

Elara's hand clenched around the ornate railing, her knuckles turning white. The weight of the crown felt heavier than ever, as if it was made of lead, a symbol of everything that had gone wrong in her life. She had inherited not only the throne but the curse that had plagued her family for generations. The ancient ones had created it, bound it to the very blood that ran through her veins. And now, that same blood would either save her or destroy everything she loved.

"Your Majesty," a voice called from behind her, pulling her from her thoughts.

Turning slowly, Elara saw her most trusted advisor, Rhiannon, approaching. Rhiannon had been with her since the early days of her reign, a constant presence in the shifting tides of the court's intrigue. But there was a weight in her eyes now, something Elara had never seen before.

"What is it, Rhiannon?" Elara's voice was steady, though the unease in her chest made her words feel hollow.

Rhiannon stepped closer, her gaze flickering toward the horizon before returning to Elara. "The council is growing restless. They speak of your father's illness, of the bloodline's curse. There are those who fear it will claim you, as it did him."

Elara's jaw tightened. She had expected this, of course, but it did nothing to ease the sting. "They are wrong," she said, her voice sharp. "The curse will not claim me. I will find a way to break it."

Rhiannon looked at her, her expression unreadable. "And if you cannot?" she asked quietly.

The question hung in the air, heavy and suffocating. Elara didn't answer immediately. What could she say? She had no answers, only the gnawing fear that the curse was closing in on her, just as it had with her father. The whispers were growing louder, the visions more vivid. And she knew, deep in her bones, that there was something waiting for her in the darkness — something ancient, powerful, and beyond her control.

"I will break it," Elara repeated, her voice stronger this time, though it was laced with uncertainty. "I will find the temple in my dreams. The one where the answers lie. I will do whatever it takes."

Rhiannon nodded, though Elara could see the hesitation in her eyes. "I will stand with you, Your Majesty. But you must be prepared. The path ahead is fraught with dangers you cannot yet imagine."

Elara nodded, her gaze returning to the dark expanse before her. The path ahead would be treacherous, that much was certain. But she had no choice. The curse had been placed upon her family by the ancients, and now it was her turn to face it. To either destroy it or be consumed by it.

She took a deep breath, steadying herself against the storm of doubt and fear that threatened to overtake her. The legacy of the Bloodborn was one of power, but it was also one of sacrifice. Elara would have to decide what she was willing to lose to save her kingdom — and her soul.

As she turned away from the balcony and walked back into the dimly lit corridors of the castle, she knew that her journey had only just begun. The curse of the ancients would not be broken easily, but she would not let it define her. Not now, not ever.

The queen was ready to face her fate.

Elara's footsteps echoed through the cold stone halls of the castle as she made her way to the war room. The weight of her thoughts pressed heavily upon her, each step feeling as if it led her deeper into the abyss of uncertainty. The ancient curse that had bound her family for centuries seemed to be closing in, and with every passing day, it grew harder to deny the truth.

As she entered the war room, the flickering torchlight cast long shadows across the large wooden table at the center. The council had gathered, their faces grim, their murmurs hushed as Elara took her seat. Her mind was elsewhere, however. The dream from the previous night still haunted her — the vision of the temple buried deep beneath the earth, the whispers in the language of the ancients, and the haunting eyes of her ancestors, pleading with her to understand. But the more she tried to grasp the meaning, the more elusive it became.

Rhiannon, standing at the edge of the room, watched her with an unreadable expression. Elara could feel the weight of her gaze but refused to let it falter her. She had to remain strong, for her people, for her kingdom, and for herself.

"Your Majesty," Lord Jarek's voice cut through her reverie, his tone respectful yet laced with concern. "The matter of your father's illness grows worse by the day. The people whisper that the curse is taking hold of the throne. You must act swiftly, or we risk losing the confidence of the kingdom."

Elara raised her chin, meeting Jarek's eyes with determination. "I am aware of the situation, Lord Jarek. But the curse will not control me. I will find the way to break it."

"Even if it means risking everything?" Lady Isolde asked, her voice low but sharp. She had always been wary of Elara's boldness, but there was a flicker of something else in her eyes now — fear, perhaps, or something darker.

Elara did not hesitate. "Yes. I will risk everything. The ancients left us clues, and I will follow them, no matter the cost."

The room fell silent. The others exchanged uneasy glances, unsure of how to proceed. The curse was not something they could easily dismiss, not something they could ignore. It had ravaged their family for generations, and now, it threatened to consume their queen.

"I'll help you," Rhiannon spoke softly, stepping forward. "But I fear the path you seek will not be one of salvation. The ancients were not merciful. They did not give up their secrets lightly."

Elara nodded, acknowledging Rhiannon's wisdom. "I know, but I have no choice. This kingdom, my people, they depend on me. If I fail, everything will be lost."

"Then we must prepare," Lord Jarek said, his tone resolute. "We cannot let this curse claim you as it did your father. We must find the temple — wherever it may be — and uncover the ancient knowledge it holds. If there is a way to break the curse, we will find it."

Elara's gaze swept over the council, meeting the eyes of each of her advisors. She could see the doubt in their eyes, the fear of the unknown, but she also saw something else — determination, a willingness to stand by her side, even in the face of an ancient evil.

"Gather the best scouts and trackers in the kingdom," Elara ordered. "We will begin the search for the temple. We must find it before the curse consumes us all."

The council members nodded, their faces set with resolve. As they began to disperse and make preparations, Elara turned to Rhiannon.

"Prepare yourself, Rhiannon. We leave at dawn."

Rhiannon gave a small nod. "I will be ready, Your Majesty. But I warn you, the path ahead is fraught with dangers beyond your imagining."

Elara smiled grimly. "I've faced worse."

As the castle descended into the quiet of the night, Elara stood alone in the war room for a moment longer, staring at the maps spread across the table. The quest for the temple would not be easy. The ancient curse that had claimed her ancestors was a force unlike any she had ever encountered. But she could not afford to fail.

She would not fail.

The fate of her bloodline, her kingdom, and her very soul depended on the choices she made in the coming days. The curse had plagued her family for centuries, but it would end with her. She would be the one to break it, or she would be consumed by it.

And in that moment, standing on the precipice of destiny, Elara knew that the storm ahead would test everything she was. But she would not be a passive player in the story of her life. She would fight for her future, for her people, and for the truth that had been hidden by the ancients.

The curse of the ancients had come for her, but Elara was ready to meet it head-on.

- The Bloodline's Dark Secret

Elara stood before the ancient mirror, her reflection fractured by the faintest ripple of moonlight that slipped through the heavy curtains. The chamber was thick with silence, the kind that pressed on her chest, making each breath feel heavier than the last. In the stillness, the whispers of the past seemed to hum around her, tugging at the edges of her thoughts.

She reached for the worn leather-bound book on the table beside her, its pages yellowed with age. The Bloodborn Chronicles were a history she had been taught to fear, but now, with the weight of the crown heavy upon her brow, Elara knew she could no longer ignore it. The secrets of her lineage, the ancient bloodline that ran through her veins, had always been shrouded in mystery. But as the days grew darker and her enemies more cunning, it was clear that the time had come to confront them.

The book opened to a page marked by a scarlet ribbon, the ink faded but still legible. Her fingers trembled as she read the words that had been passed down through generations of rulers.

"The blood of the ancient ones is both a gift and a curse. It binds those who inherit it to a fate they cannot escape. The power within will either destroy them or save them, but never without cost."

Her heart thudded painfully in her chest. This was the secret she had always feared—a secret that had haunted the throne for centuries. The blood that flowed through her veins, the blood of kings and queens long past, was more than just royal. It was tainted with the magic of an age forgotten, a magic that carried a price too steep for most to pay.

Elara had spent years building alliances, securing her power, and pushing back against the forces that sought to take her throne. But in all of her calculations, she had overlooked the one thing that could undo everything—the bloodline's true nature.

Her thoughts flickered to the elders, those who had raised her in the shadow of the throne. They had always spoken in riddles, cryptic phrases about destiny and the weight of royal blood. Now, Elara understood why they had kept their distance, why they had never spoken plainly. They had known what she was destined to face, and perhaps they had hoped she would never have to.

The weight of the crown, once a symbol of her right to rule, now felt more like a burden. The power she wielded, the strength she had built her reign on, was linked to this dark force, this secret that had been kept from her for so long. The knowledge was both a blessing and a curse. She could feel its pull within her, an almost tangible force that gnawed at the edges of her consciousness.

As she read on, the pages seemed to blur before her eyes, the words swirling as though they were alive. *"The firstborn of the bloodline will come to understand the true cost of their inheritance. They will be tested by those who seek to claim the throne, and they will find themselves standing at the crossroads of salvation and ruin."*

Elara closed the book with a sharp snap, the sound echoing in the stillness of the room. She had always known that her rule would not be without challenge, but this... This was something different. Something deeper. The very blood that made her a queen also made her vulnerable. And now, with enemies on every side, the question was no longer if she would survive, but at what cost.

The wind howled outside, rattling the windows, as if the very kingdom could feel the shift in the air. Elara's hand drifted to the pendant around her neck, a token from her mother. The same pendant her mother had worn, passed down through generations. The same pendant that had always felt like a comforting weight—until now. Now, it felt like a link to something darker, something older than her bloodline.

She knew that she could no longer ignore the truth. She had inherited not only a kingdom but also the weight of the past, a past that was steeped in blood and sacrifice. The path forward was unclear, but one thing was certain: the price of power was never easy, and she would soon find out just how much her bloodline had truly cost her.

The door to her chamber creaked open, breaking her reverie. She turned to see Rhiannon, her most trusted ally, step into the room. Her face was pale, her expression grave.

"The council has gathered," Rhiannon said softly, her eyes flicking to the book Elara held in her hands. "They are waiting for you."

Elara nodded, taking one last look at the pages before slipping the book back into its place. She had learned something vital tonight, something that would change the course of her rule. The battle for her throne was no longer just about strategy, alliances, or power. It was a fight for her very soul, and she was beginning to realize that the darkest forces might not lie outside her kingdom—but within it.

As she left the chamber, the weight of her heritage pressed on her once more, a constant reminder of the bloodline's dark secret. The future was uncertain, but Elara knew that she could no longer turn away from the truth. And whatever path she chose, the consequences would follow her for the rest of her life.

The corridors of the castle were dim, the flickering torches casting long shadows that danced along the walls. Each step Elara took felt heavier than the last, as though the very stones beneath her feet were pressing in on her. She could hear the murmurs of her council ahead, their voices a low hum, rising and falling in tension. The walls seemed to close in as she approached, the weight of her newfound knowledge growing with each step.

Rhiannon walked beside her, silent as always, but Elara could sense the unease in her companion's movements. Rhiannon had always been steadfast, a rock upon which Elara could rely, but tonight, something felt different. She had seen the change in her friend's eyes—an almost imperceptible flicker of doubt. It was as though Rhiannon, too, had begun to understand the gravity of the situation.

When they reached the council chamber, Elara's breath caught in her throat. The room was heavy with the presence of her most trusted advisors—men and women who had stood by her side through countless battles, all of whom had their own ambitions, secrets, and fears. They had watched her grow from a young, uncertain princess into a ruler, but none of them had seen what she had just uncovered.

Her gaze swept across the room, settling on the faces of those who had sworn their loyalty to her. Lord Kaelen, the general who had led her armies to victory; Lady Seris, her closest confidante, with eyes sharp enough to cut through any deception; and Lord Varek, whose loyalties were always questioned but who had proven invaluable in the past. Each one was now looking at her with the same intensity, as though sensing that something had changed.

"You've kept us waiting, Your Majesty," Lord Kaelen's voice broke the silence, a note of frustration hidden beneath his measured words.

Elara nodded, her expression unreadable. "I apologize, my lord. But the matter at hand requires more than just strategy. It requires understanding." Her words hung in the air, heavy and ominous. She could see the way they all stiffened at the implication, but none of them spoke. They were waiting for her to elaborate.

"I have learned something," Elara continued, her voice steady despite the turmoil raging inside her. "Something about our bloodline. The truth that has been hidden for generations. The power we wield is not just a gift—it is a curse. And I must confront it if I am to continue ruling."

A murmur of disbelief swept through the council, but Elara held up a hand, silencing them. "This is not a matter of mere power struggles. This is about our very survival. The enemies we face are not just external. There are forces within this kingdom, dark forces that have been waiting for this moment."

Lord Varek leaned forward, his sharp eyes narrowing. "What are you suggesting, Your Majesty? That we are surrounded by traitors?"

Elara met his gaze, unwavering. "Not traitors. Something far worse. The darkness within our bloodline has already begun to stir. And if we do not act swiftly, it will consume us all."

The room fell into silence as the weight of her words sank in. Even Rhiannon, who had always been her strongest ally, looked troubled, her brow furrowed in thought.

"How do you propose we proceed, Your Majesty?" Lady Seris spoke up, her voice cool but concerned. "This... revelation changes everything. It's not just a matter of politics. We are dealing with something far more dangerous than any of us anticipated."

Elara took a deep breath, steadying herself. "We must uncover the truth behind the curse. There are ancient texts, forgotten rituals, and hidden places that hold the key to breaking it. I will not allow this bloodline to destroy us. We will find a way to control it."

Kaelen, ever the pragmatist, crossed his arms. "And what of the enemies outside our walls? We cannot afford to waste time on ghosts and legends while our rivals gather at the gates."

Elara's gaze hardened. "The threats inside are just as real as those without. Perhaps more so. If we do not address this, no strategy or alliance will matter. We will fall."

The tension in the room was palpable, each member of the council weighing her words carefully. Finally, Lord Varek spoke again, his voice laced with skepticism but tinged with curiosity. "And what will you have us do, my queen? If this curse is as powerful as you say, it will take more than just your strength to overcome it."

Elara's gaze turned to each of them, her resolve hardening. "We will do whatever it takes. We will search for the ancient texts, seek out those who know the old ways, and uncover every hidden truth. We may not have all the answers, but together, we will find a way to control this curse before it controls us."

The room was silent for a long moment as the council members processed her words. Finally, Kaelen gave a small nod, his gaze intense. "If this is the path you choose, Your Majesty, we will follow. But you must be prepared. The road ahead will not be easy."

Elara nodded, her heart heavy but determined. "I am prepared for whatever it takes."

As the council session concluded, Elara stood in the center of the room, her mind racing. The weight of the bloodline's dark secret pressed on her, but there was no turning back now. The game had changed, and the stakes were higher than ever. Her enemies were no longer just those who sought her throne. The true enemy lay within her very blood, and it was a foe far more dangerous than any army or political rival.

She could feel it stirring within her, a power both ancient and terrible. And now, it was time to face it head-on.

Part II: The Rise of the Fallen

1. Vanguard's Return

○ The Silent Enemy

The night was eerily still as the kingdom of Eldoria lay under a blanket of thick, unrelenting fog. The air was heavy with an unsettling quiet, as if the world itself had paused, holding its breath. Elara, the Queen of Eldoria, stood on the balcony of the palace, staring out into the swirling mist. Her thoughts were as turbulent as the weather, though the rest of the kingdom appeared to be asleep. It had been years since she had felt such a pervasive sense of dread. Her enemies were numerous, but this time, there was something different in the air—a silent force gathering in the shadows, watching, waiting.

The first whispers had come weeks ago, a murmur among her spies, barely audible at first. Then, as days passed, the news had grown more urgent. There was something—or someone—lurking in the dark corners of the kingdom, something Elara couldn't see but felt deep in her bones. It wasn't just an external enemy; it was an enemy that had been growing within, silent and unseen, biding its time.

In the dimly lit war room, Elara sat at a long, oak table, her fingers tracing the edges of a map. Her trusted lieutenant, Rhiannon, stood by her side, a grim expression on her face. The two women had fought side by side through countless battles, yet Rhiannon's unease was palpable now, a stark contrast to her usually unshakable composure.

"Elara, I fear the enemy we face is not one we can easily defeat with swords and shields," Rhiannon said quietly, her voice low as though she were afraid someone might overhear.

Elara turned her gaze to her lieutenant. "What do you mean?"

Rhiannon hesitated, her eyes flickering to the door as if she feared being overheard. "It's not just the rebels or the Vanguard. There's something older. Something... darker. The enemy that stirs now is not flesh and bone. It is something far more insidious, something that can only be defeated with the mind, not the sword."

A shiver ran down Elara's spine. She had long known that the fight for the throne wasn't solely about military might, but she hadn't prepared herself for an enemy she couldn't see, couldn't touch. Something beyond the realm of politics, beyond even the magic she wielded.

"This enemy..." Elara whispered, her voice barely audible. "Who is it?"

Rhiannon shook her head, her expression tense. "I do not know yet, but I feel its presence in every corner of this palace. There are whispers of dark rituals, of forbidden pacts being made in the shadows. People are disappearing, soldiers are acting strangely, and rumors of a powerful sorcerer in hiding have reached my ears. Whoever—or whatever—this enemy is, it is no mere mortal. It is something that feeds off fear, that grows stronger the more we ignore it."

Elara's hand tightened around the map as she processed Rhiannon's words. This was more than just a political threat—it was a force that could unravel everything she had fought for, everything she had built. Her kingdom, her people, her own very life were all at risk. And yet, despite the looming danger, there was no tangible enemy to strike at, no general to lead her army against. The battle had become something far more elusive, a battle of wills, a contest of minds in a game she had yet to fully understand.

"We will find it," Elara said with quiet resolve, her voice filled with an icy determination. "We will root out this silent enemy before it is too late. We must remain vigilant."

Rhiannon nodded, her gaze fixed on Elara. "The darkness is growing, Your Majesty. You must act quickly."

As Elara turned back to the map, her mind raced. There were many places to search, many paths to explore, but one thing was clear—whoever or whatever this silent enemy was, it would not remain hidden for much longer. And when it finally emerged, the battle would be unlike any she had ever fought before.

With one last glance at Rhiannon, Elara stood, a fire igniting in her chest. It was time to strike before the enemy could strike first. And this time, it would not be through force of arms, but through the quiet, deliberate precision of her own mind.

The game had changed, and Elara was ready to play.

The days that followed were filled with a growing sense of urgency. Elara knew that every hour spent in hesitation could bring the kingdom closer to the precipice. Her mind turned over every possible lead, every potential threat, searching for clues in the silence that seemed to stretch endlessly before her. The walls of the palace had become her only refuge, but even here, she could feel the weight of the unseen presence lurking just beyond reach.

Rhiannon had been busy, gathering intel from her network of spies and informants. But the more they dug, the less they found. The shadowy figures who had once moved through the kingdom's underworld seemed to have vanished, leaving only whispers of their passing. It was as though the kingdom itself had been consumed by a dark veil, suffocating everything in its path.

One evening, as Elara paced the war room, her fingers tracing the edges of ancient tomes, she heard a soft knock at the door. Rhiannon entered, her face ashen, her eyes wide with fear. The lieutenant was usually the picture of composure, but today, there was something different about her—something unnerving.

"Speak," Elara commanded, her voice sharp.

Rhiannon hesitated, a flicker of doubt crossing her face. "There have been reports, Your Majesty. Rumors of an ancient cult, one thought lost to time. They call themselves the Silent Order."

Elara's heart skipped a beat. The name sent chills down her spine. She had heard whispers of the Silent Order, though she had long believed them to be nothing more than a myth, a shadow in the pages of forgotten history. It was said they had once wielded power beyond imagination, manipulating the very fabric of magic itself, but they had vanished centuries ago, leaving only cryptic records behind.

"What do they want?" Elara asked, her mind already working through the possibilities.

"We don't know," Rhiannon replied, her voice barely a whisper. "But there are rumors they've resurfaced, that they've found a way to bring their power back. And they're operating from the shadows, just as we feared."

Elara's grip on the edge of the table tightened. The Silent Order—if they were truly behind this—could spell the end of everything she had worked for. Their methods were not like those of the ordinary rebels or political enemies she had faced in the past. The Silent Order was a different kind of adversary—one that knew how to strike from the darkness, sowing fear and confusion in their wake.

"We need more information," Elara said, her voice filled with steely determination. "Rhiannon, gather every piece of intel you can on this order. Find out who's leading them, where they're hiding, and how they intend to bring their power back. This is no longer a matter of just securing my throne. It's about saving the kingdom."

Rhiannon nodded, her expression grim. "At once, Your Majesty."

As the lieutenant departed, Elara's thoughts turned inward. The Silent Order was no ordinary enemy. They had the power to slip through the cracks, to blend into the very fabric of society, leaving no trace of their existence. They were the epitome of the silent enemy, lurking in the shadows, waiting for the perfect moment to strike.

Elara knew that time was running out. She had to act quickly, before this unseen enemy could tighten its grip on the kingdom. But how could she fight an enemy she couldn't see, an enemy whose very nature made it impossible to confront with conventional means?

The answers were elusive, but one thing was certain—Elara would not stand idly by and let her kingdom fall into the hands of those who operated in the dark. She would find them. She would confront them. And she would stop them, no matter the cost.

As the fog outside thickened, so too did the weight of Elara's resolve. She was no longer just a queen, fighting to protect her throne. She was a leader facing an existential threat, one that required every ounce of her cunning, strength, and will to defeat.

The Silent Enemy may have been lurking in the shadows, but Elara would drag it into the light. She would uncover the truth, no matter how deep she had to dig. And when she did, she would ensure that it would be the enemy who would remain silent forever.

○ A Lost Battle Reborn

The cold wind whipped through the barren plains, carrying the scent of blood and ash. In the distance, the remnants of an ancient battlefield lay scattered, the once proud banners of the fallen kingdoms now tattered and forgotten. The earth beneath Elara's boots seemed to tremble, as if the very land itself had witnessed the horrors of war and refused to forget.

She stood still, her cloak billowing in the wind, her eyes narrowed in contemplation. The day was coming when the history of this place would no longer be buried in the past. The battle fought here, long ago, had been a turning point—a battle that should have been the end, but had only marked the beginning of something far darker.

Behind her, the army of the Bloodborn was ready. Soldiers from all corners of the kingdom, drawn together by a common cause, stood at attention, their eyes fixed on their queen. They were eager for the coming war, eager for revenge against those who had wronged them, who had betrayed them.

But Elara knew that this would not be a simple fight. No, this was more than just another battle. It was a rebirth, a reckoning. The blood of those who had fallen here, centuries ago, still ran deep in the earth, calling to her, whispering of vengeance. This land was not just the site of a lost battle; it was the birthplace of a war that had yet to be fully fought. And she, as the heir to that bloodline, would be the one to finish it.

Her hand rested on the hilt of her sword, the blade gleaming with a light that was both ethereal and dangerous. She had come here for a reason. The time had come to reawaken the forgotten powers that had lain dormant for so long. The enemy she had been hunting—Vanguard—was not a new force. They had been here long before, hiding in the shadows, biding their time. Now, they had returned. And Elara would not rest until they were crushed beneath her heel.

She turned to face her commanders, her voice carrying across the field, calm but resolute. "Today, we honor the fallen. Today, we reclaim what was lost."

The soldiers cheered, a fierce, unified cry rising from their throats. But Elara's gaze lingered on the horizon. She could feel it—something stirring, something ancient awakening beneath her feet.

The battle had been lost once, but it would not be lost again. Not with her at the helm.

As the army advanced, the first clash of steel against steel echoed across the plains, reverberating through the centuries. The ground shook as if in response, and the skies darkened with the promise of the storm to come.

This was no ordinary fight. It was the birth of a new war, one that would shape the fate of all who stood upon this cursed land. And Elara, the queen with the blood of warriors flowing through her veins, would be the one to see it through to its bitter end.

The past was not forgotten—it had merely been waiting for its moment to rise again.

The clash of steel continued, a symphony of violence and rage, as Elara led her forces forward with unwavering determination. The battlefield seemed to come alive with every swing of a blade, every scream of a soldier, and every footstep that echoed through the smoke-filled air. But amid the chaos, Elara's focus remained sharp, her mind clear. She had fought many battles in her life, but none felt as personal as this one. This was not just a fight for her kingdom; it was a fight for her bloodline, a fight to prove that the past, however dark, could be turned into a weapon for the future.

As the lines between her soldiers and Vanguard's forces blurred, Elara spotted a figure in the distance. Tall, cloaked in shadows, and moving with an eerie grace, the figure seemed to glide across the battlefield, untouched by the carnage around it. Elara's breath caught in her throat. She knew that presence. It was him.

"Gaius," she whispered under her breath.

Gaius, the leader of Vanguard, the man who had once been her closest ally, had become her greatest enemy. His betrayal had shattered her trust and turned him into a living nightmare. His return meant only one thing: the final confrontation was at hand.

With a quick motion, Elara signaled to her closest commanders. They knew the drill. The battle raged around them, but the real fight would take place between her and Gaius. She knew the risks—he was as skilled with a blade as she was, if not more so—but this time, it was different. This time, it wasn't just their lives at stake. The fate of the entire kingdom rested on the outcome of this duel.

Elara pushed through the chaos, her movements a blur of practiced precision. She could hear the sounds of battle fade into the background as she focused on her target. Gaius's eyes met hers from across the battlefield, and for a brief moment, time seemed to slow. The air crackled with tension, as if the world itself was holding its breath in anticipation of the storm that was about to come.

When they finally stood face to face, the noise of the battlefield seemed to vanish entirely. Only the two of them remained in this space, locked in a gaze that spoke of old wounds and unfinished business.

"You've come to finish what we started, Elara?" Gaius's voice was cold, like the steel of the blade he held in his hand. "Or are you simply here to die?"

Elara's hand tightened around the hilt of her sword, the weight of her purpose settling in her chest. "No, Gaius. I'm here to end this."

Without another word, they clashed.

The sound of their swords meeting echoed like thunder, a sharp, metallic ring that reverberated through the air. Elara's strength was matched by Gaius's, each blow a test of skill and resolve. Their movements were a blur, each strike and parry a dance they had once shared in a different time, under different circumstances. But there was no camaraderie now, only the raw, brutal desire for victory.

Gaius's eyes gleamed with a dark satisfaction. "You've always been a fool, Elara. You never understood that the true power lies in control. In ruling from the shadows."

"You were never meant to rule, Gaius," Elara shot back, her voice fierce. "You were meant to protect. But you chose to betray everything we stood for."

Their swords collided once more, and Elara felt a sharp sting as Gaius's blade grazed her arm. She hissed in pain but didn't falter. The blood that dripped from her wound only fueled her resolve. This was the moment she had been waiting for—the moment to end the betrayal, to avenge her fallen comrades, to take back what was rightfully hers.

With a fierce cry, Elara launched herself at Gaius, her sword a blur of deadly precision. She struck, again and again, each blow pushing him back. Gaius faltered for the first time, his arrogance finally beginning to crack.

But Gaius was not done. With a savage roar, he swung his blade in a wild arc, aiming for Elara's head. She blocked just in time, the force of the blow sending a shockwave through her body. For a moment, they stood there, panting, eyes locked in mutual hatred. Blood stained the ground beneath them, a symbol of the years they had both lost to war and treachery.

"You won't win this time," Elara said, her voice low but filled with conviction. "This is the last battle, Gaius. The last reckoning."

For a moment, Gaius hesitated. There was a flicker of something in his eyes, something almost human. But it was gone as quickly as it had appeared, replaced by the cold, calculating demeanor he had worn for so long.

"This is not the end," Gaius said, a twisted smile creeping across his face. "This is just the beginning."

But Elara didn't give him the chance to finish. With one final, powerful swing, she drove her sword deep into his chest, silencing his words and ending the life of the man who had once been her greatest ally.

As Gaius crumpled to the ground, Elara stood over him, breathless and covered in blood. The battle raged on around her, but in that moment, she felt a sense of peace. The past had been laid to rest. The future was now hers to claim.

And with the death of Gaius, the rebirth of the lost battle had been completed. The kingdom was one step closer to its salvation.

But Elara knew the war was far from over.

- The First Confrontation

The air was thick with tension as the two armies lined up across the barren field. The dust from the last few days of rain still clung to the earth, an unsettling reminder of the bloodshed that had yet to come. Elara stood at the forefront, her eyes scanning the horizon, where a storm of smoke and fire was beginning to rise. The Vanguard had arrived, and with them, an old enemy—one she had hoped to never face again.

Her fingers tightened around the hilt of her sword. The blade, once a symbol of hope and unity, now felt heavy, as though the weight of the world rested on its edge. Her heart pounded, not just with the anticipation of battle, but with the growing realization that this confrontation was no ordinary fight. It was personal.

Across the field, standing in the midst of the Vanguard's ranks, was a figure that haunted her nightmares: Valerian, her former ally, now turned enemy. The betrayal was still fresh in her mind, a wound that had never fully healed. He had once been her confidant, her closest friend. Together, they had fought side by side, believing in a future where their kingdom would rise above its enemies. But that dream had shattered the moment Valerian had made his choice—the moment he had turned his back on her, on the crown, and on everything they had fought for.

His eyes locked with hers from across the battlefield, a cold smirk curling his lips. The years between them had only deepened the divide, but the hatred in his gaze was unmistakable. Elara could feel the blood rushing to her face, her anger rising like an inferno ready to consume everything in its path. But she couldn't afford to let that anger control her—not now, not here.

"Steady, Your Majesty," Rhiannon's voice was a calm presence beside her. The witch had remained loyal, even when many others had turned their backs on the queen. Elara looked at her, the woman's knowing eyes offering silent reassurance.

"I know," Elara muttered, though the words felt hollow. She knew that the stakes of this battle went far beyond her personal vendetta. It was about the survival of her kingdom, the preservation of everything they had worked for. She couldn't afford to lose herself in the past, no matter how bitter it tasted.

The horn sounded, a deep, resonant call that echoed across the land, signaling the beginning of the clash. The Vanguard surged forward, their heavy footsteps shaking the earth beneath them. Elara raised her sword high, her heart steadying in the face of the inevitable. The time for talk was over.

She spurred her horse forward, the sound of hooves thundering in her ears as she led her army into the fray. The battlefield erupted into chaos, the clash of metal on metal ringing through the air like a symphony of destruction. Elara's sword met the first of the Vanguard's soldiers with brutal force, cutting through the air in a fluid, deadly arc. She didn't stop to look at her fallen enemy; her gaze was fixed on Valerian, who was still standing at the rear, watching her approach with unnerving calm.

The ground seemed to tremble beneath their feet as they closed the distance. And then, with no further words, no final plea, it was just them—Elara and Valerian, face to face once more.

"You should have stayed out of this, Elara," Valerian's voice was low, yet it cut through the din of battle like a knife. "You could have had it all. You could have ruled without bloodshed."

"I don't want to rule with your kind of power," she shot back, her voice unwavering. "The throne isn't worth sacrificing everything for."

His laugh was cold, devoid of any warmth. "Then you're already lost."

In that moment, time seemed to slow. The chaos around them faded as their world became only the two of them—two people who had once fought for the same cause, now on opposite sides of a war neither of them had wanted, but both had been forced into.

Elara's sword came down with a sharp, calculated strike. Valerian parried it effortlessly, their blades clashing with a sound that could only be described as the ringing of destiny. They fought like two seasoned warriors, each blow they exchanged carrying the weight of years of pain, betrayal, and regret.

"You were always too weak," Valerian taunted, pressing his attack. "You never had the strength to do what needed to be done."

Elara's grip tightened, her resolve hardening. "And yet, I'm still standing."

The battle around them raged on, but in that moment, it was just the two of them—fated to face each other in the last, inevitable confrontation. Neither could back down, not now. Not with everything on the line.

Each strike, each block, was more than just a fight for survival—it was the reckoning of a friendship lost, the final judgment of everything they had once stood for.

Their swords clashed again, sparks flying from the force of the blow. The energy between them crackled, heavy with the history they shared. Elara could feel the weight of Valerian's hatred in every strike, but there was something more in his eyes—something darker, more desperate. It wasn't just anger; it was fear. Fear that he had made the wrong choice, but too proud to admit it.

For a fleeting moment, Elara thought she saw a flicker of hesitation in him, as if the man she had once known—the man who had stood beside her in battle—was still there beneath the cold armor of a traitor. But it was gone as quickly as it had appeared, swallowed up by the storm of rage that consumed him.

"You never understood, did you?" Valerian spat, his voice laced with venom. "This isn't about power. It's about survival. You were always too blinded by your ideals, too soft."

Elara's grip tightened on the hilt of her sword. "And you were always too eager to sacrifice others for your own gain. That's what makes you weak, Valerian. You don't understand what it means to lead, to protect. You only know how to destroy."

His eyes burned with fury. "You think you're any different? The throne corrupts everyone. You'll see that soon enough. You'll become just like me."

Elara's heart raced, but she forced herself to focus. His words were nothing more than poison meant to sow doubt, to break her resolve. She couldn't afford to let him drag her down to his level. She had to finish this, for herself and for the kingdom.

With a swift, fluid movement, she spun her blade to deflect his next strike, and in that split second of vulnerability, she took her chance. Elara's sword found its mark, a clean cut across Valerian's chest. He staggered back, his breath catching as the blood stained the once-gleaming armor he wore.

For a moment, the battlefield around them seemed to pause, the chaos fading into the background as Elara stood over him, her sword raised. Valerian looked up at her, his eyes wide with shock and pain, but there was something else there too—something she couldn't quite place. Regret? Fear? Perhaps a mix of both.

"You... you were always too good for this," Valerian whispered, his voice strained. His breath was shallow, the blood pouring from his wound, but his gaze remained fixed on her. "I... I wanted to make it better. I thought... I thought I could change everything."

Elara's heart clenched at his words, but she couldn't allow herself to be swayed. Not now. Not after everything. She had once believed in him, trusted him with everything, but that trust had been broken long ago. She had to be the queen now. The ruler her people needed.

"You made your choice," she said coldly, her voice unwavering. "And now you'll face the consequences."

Valerian didn't respond. His head fell back, and his body slumped to the ground, the life leaving him as swiftly as the winds that swept across the battlefield.

Elara stood over him, her heart heavy with the weight of what she had just done. The fight was far from over, but this—this moment—felt like the end of something more personal. She had killed a friend. She had killed a part of herself.

The sounds of battle returned as her soldiers pushed forward, forcing the Vanguard back. Elara's eyes swept across the field, noting the wounded, the fallen. Her mind raced, but she could not allow herself to grieve. Not yet. There was still a war to win.

With a deep breath, she turned away from Valerian's lifeless body. Her eyes hardened as they found the distant horizon, where the next wave of enemies awaited. The confrontation with Valerian had been inevitable, but it was just the beginning. The true battle for her kingdom was far from over.

"We've won this round," Rhiannon said softly, coming up beside her. "But the war is far from finished."

Elara nodded, her face set in grim determination. "I know. And I'll fight to the end. For them. For the people who still believe in us."

She mounted her horse, her gaze never leaving the battlefield. Her army rallied behind her, ready to press on. They had been through too much, sacrificed too much, to let this war end in failure. The path ahead would be fraught with more betrayals, more bloodshed. But Elara was no longer the uncertain queen who had begun this journey. She was a leader, forged in the crucible of war, tempered by loss.

And she would not stop until her kingdom was free.

2. The Witch's Mark

○ Rhiannon's Revelation

Rhiannon stood at the edge of the cliff, the wind howling through the jagged rocks, her silver hair whipping around her face like a storm. The night was thick with shadows, the moonlight barely breaking through the dense clouds that gathered ominously above. She had always known that something was hidden within the fabric of her past, something she had yet to understand. Tonight, however, the pieces of the puzzle would finally fall into place.

She had spent years running from the truth, burying her feelings under layers of misdirection, pretending to be content with the path she had chosen. But the truth, like a hidden fire beneath the earth's surface, had a way of rising when least expected. Rhiannon could feel it now, a deep, unsettling pull inside her that demanded her attention. She closed her eyes, willing herself to remain calm, even as her heart pounded in her chest.

The ancient stones before her seemed to hum with an energy that was foreign to her, yet familiar. She had crossed this threshold many times before, but never in this state of mind, never with the weight of what she had learned on her shoulders. Rhiannon had always been a woman of power, of vision, but even she was not immune to the revelations that lay in wait for those who dared to uncover the truth.

The whispers began softly, barely a murmur against the wind. They spoke in a language forgotten by most, a language of power, of blood, and of old alliances that spanned centuries. At first, Rhiannon could not make out the words. They seemed to slip through her mind like water through fingers, elusive and distant. But then, something changed. A sharpness to the whispers, an urgency that made her skin crawl.

It was then that the truth, hidden for so long, revealed itself in its full, chilling clarity. The prophecy, the bloodline, the ancient curse—everything was interwoven in a pattern too complex to be mere coincidence. Rhiannon's ancestors, those she had once believed to be mere legends, were not only real but had been key players in shaping the very fate of the kingdom. The magic she had always felt within her, the power she had wielded so easily, was not of her own making. It was inherited, passed down through generations, bound by blood and shadow.

Her mother, long dead, had been part of the secret that Rhiannon had been unknowingly drawn into. Her true legacy, her purpose, had been hidden from her for her entire life. And now, in this moment, Rhiannon understood the depth of her role in the coming war. She was not just a healer, a leader, or a sorceress. She was the key to an ancient conflict that would determine the fate of all.

But with this revelation came a heavy burden. The truth was never without cost. The power that flowed through her veins was not something to be taken lightly. It demanded sacrifices, and Rhiannon could already feel the weight of what was to come pressing against her chest. She had always known that her destiny was larger than the simple life she had envisioned, but she had never truly understood what that meant until now.

A vision flashed before her eyes, brief but vivid. A battlefield, stained with blood. Figures—familiar faces—fighting, dying, and in the center, a woman with eyes like hers, standing amidst the chaos, making a choice that would shape the future. The vision faded as quickly as it had appeared, leaving her breathless and shaken.

Rhiannon opened her eyes and exhaled slowly, trying to steady herself. The wind howled louder, as if urging her to make her decision, to embrace what she had just learned. The road ahead was not one she could walk alone, but even as doubt crept into her thoughts, she knew that there was no turning back.

With a final glance at the cliffs below, she turned away, her mind already racing with the implications of what she had learned. Her revelation had marked the beginning of a new chapter, one that would force her to confront her past, her bloodline, and her true place in the coming war. The world was shifting beneath her feet, and Rhiannon could feel the tremors in her very bones.

The time for secrets had passed.

Rhiannon's footsteps echoed in the silent night as she walked away from the cliff's edge. The revelation had unsettled her, but it also ignited a fierce determination within her. She could no longer deny the truth of her bloodline, nor the role she was meant to play in the coming storm. Her destiny had always been written in the stars, and now, for the first time, she truly understood the weight of those words.

The moon hung low in the sky, its pale light casting long shadows across the land. Rhiannon could feel the presence of something ancient around her, as though the earth itself was alive, watching, waiting. It was the magic, the old power that thrummed through her veins, that seemed to breathe in rhythm with the world. The more she embraced it, the stronger she felt, but with that strength came a foreboding sense of responsibility.

Her mind raced as she thought back to the fragments of the prophecy—the whispered words she had overheard in the hidden chambers of the temple. There was more to uncover, more to understand. She couldn't rely on the visions alone; she needed answers. But where to start?

Rhiannon had always been resourceful, always able to find the path when others faltered. Yet, this was different. This was not just about her own survival or the survival of her people—it was about something far greater. She had glimpsed the future, and the price of victory was yet to be revealed.

As she reached the edge of the village, the familiar sight of the stone houses and bustling marketplace felt strange to her now. She had lived among these people her entire life, yet she knew they were unaware of the forces at play behind closed doors. The village was only a small piece of a much larger puzzle, and for the first time, Rhiannon felt as though she was standing outside it, looking in.

Her thoughts were interrupted by the sudden appearance of a shadow in the street. She stiffened, her hand instinctively reaching for the hilt of her dagger, though she quickly relaxed as she recognized the figure. It was Kaelen, her most trusted confidant and long-time friend.

"You're back late," Kaelen said, his voice low but laced with concern. His eyes flicked toward her, searching for any signs of distress. "Are you alright?"

Rhiannon took a deep breath, still feeling the weight of the revelation pressing down on her. "I'm fine," she said, though her voice lacked conviction. She wasn't sure if she would ever feel fine again. "I've learned something—something that changes everything."

Kaelen raised an eyebrow, his expression shifting from concern to curiosity. "What is it?"

Rhiannon hesitated for a moment, weighing her words. She had always been careful with Kaelen, knowing how much he cared for her, how deeply he was invested in her well-being. But this—this was something that could alter the course of their lives forever. She wasn't sure if he was ready to hear it.

"The prophecy," she began slowly, her gaze drifting toward the horizon as if the words might be easier to say to the stars than to him. "It's real. And I—"

"You're the one it speaks of," Kaelen finished for her, his voice barely a whisper.

Rhiannon looked at him, startled by how easily he had deduced her meaning. "How did you know?"

He shrugged, his expression unreadable. "I've always known there was more to you than you let on. There's power in you, Rhiannon. I've seen it in the way you move, the way you think. You've always carried something heavy, something that sets you apart. I didn't want to believe it, but now..." He paused, his gaze hardening. "Now it makes sense."

Rhiannon nodded, a chill running down her spine as Kaelen's words echoed in her mind. He was right. She had always known that there was more to her than met the eye, but she had never fully understood what that "more" was.

"You've got to prepare yourself," Kaelen continued, his tone serious. "There's no running from this, no hiding. If you're truly the one in the prophecy, then you'll need more than just your magic. You'll need allies. You'll need to know who you can trust, and who might betray you."

Rhiannon felt a surge of determination rise within her. Kaelen was right, of course. She couldn't face this alone, not with the stakes so high. But even as she acknowledged the truth of his words, a part of her recoiled. The future she had seen was not one she would have chosen. But it was hers nonetheless.

"I'll need to find the others," she said, more to herself than to Kaelen. "The ones mentioned in the prophecy. The ones who will help me fight."

Kaelen nodded, his gaze softening. "You're not alone, Rhiannon. Whatever happens, I'll be by your side."

Her heart clenched at the sincerity in his voice. She didn't want to drag him into this world of blood and magic, but she knew he was right—she would need him, perhaps more than she realized.

Rhiannon stood tall, her eyes fixed on the path ahead. There was no turning back now. The prophecy had been revealed, and with it, her fate had been sealed. All that was left was to walk the road, wherever it might lead, and face whatever challenges lay ahead.

The wind picked up once more, carrying with it a sense of finality. It was as if the world itself was pushing her forward, urging her to embrace the truth, to wield the power she had been born to command.

And as Rhiannon set off into the night, her heart filled with resolve, she knew one thing for certain: she would never be the same again.

○ The Ancient Rites

The night had fallen heavy over the kingdom, a blanket of shadows that seemed to seep into every corner of the castle. The cold stone walls of the chamber echoed with the sound of Elara's measured footsteps as she approached the altar. The air was thick with the scent of incense, a blend of herbs and sacred oils that filled the space with an unsettling calm. The flickering light of a single torch cast dancing shadows across the ancient symbols carved into the stone floor, a stark reminder of the blood rituals that had shaped her ancestors.

Elara's heart raced in her chest, a heavy thrum that seemed to drown out all other sounds. She had come to this place before, in the dead of night when the kingdom slept and the weight of her crown felt unbearably heavy. But tonight was different. Tonight, she was here not out of duty, but out of desperation. The whispers had grown louder, the prophecy pressing down on her like a vice, and the dark power that flowed through her veins was beginning to stir. She could feel it—growing stronger with each passing day, threatening to overwhelm her if she didn't find a way to control it.

The ancient rites were the only path left. The blood of her ancestors, the very same blood that had cursed her family line, was now her only salvation. But there were risks. The ritual was dangerous, its outcome uncertain. Many had attempted it in the past, only to be consumed by the dark forces they sought to control. But what choice did she have? The kingdom was on the brink of war, and the shadows that had once been allies were now her enemies. She could no longer afford to be weak.

With trembling hands, she placed a single silver chalice on the altar. Its surface was etched with the same symbols that adorned the floor, a map of her ancestors' legacy. Elara's eyes flickered over the chalice, the weight of her decision pressing heavily on her. This was the moment when everything would change.

She lifted the chalice and turned her gaze to the stone walls. The ancient rites required more than just the offering of blood; they required a pact with the darkness itself. A pact that would bind her forever to the forces she sought to command. But in doing so, she would gain the power to protect her kingdom, to defend her people from the very forces that sought to destroy them.

The incantations were ancient, their meaning lost to time, but Elara knew them by heart. She had recited them a thousand times in her mind, each word a thread weaving her fate with that of the kingdom. The air in the chamber seemed to grow thicker as she began, her voice steady as she spoke the words of the ritual.

The first drop of blood fell into the chalice, a sharp pain shooting through her palm. But it was nothing compared to the storm that began to swirl around her. The torches flickered violently, their flames stretching upward as if reaching for something just out of their grasp. The air grew colder, and the shadows seemed to move, shifting and writhing like living creatures.

Elara's pulse quickened as the darkness began to take shape. She could feel it now, the power coursing through her, its presence like a weight pressing down on her chest. The ritual was taking hold.

A voice, low and guttural, whispered from the shadows. "You have come to us, Queen. What is it that you seek?"

Her breath caught in her throat. She had known this moment would come, but to hear it—so real, so tangible—was a shock. The voice was not of this world. It was ancient, older than the very stones that surrounded her. The blood of her ancestors had awakened it, and now she stood on the precipice of something far greater than she had ever imagined.

"I seek the power to protect my kingdom," Elara replied, her voice unwavering despite the fear that gripped her heart. "To save it from the darkness that threatens to consume it."

The shadows whispered in response, their voice a low murmur that seemed to come from all directions at once. "And what will you offer in return, Queen?"

Elara's gaze hardened. She had already made the choice, and she knew the cost. She could feel the power calling to her, a seductive force that promised strength and dominion, but at a price.

"I offer my soul," she said, her words carrying the weight of finality. "I offer my very life, if that is what is required."

The shadows stilled. For a moment, there was silence, as if the darkness itself was weighing her words. Then, the voice spoke again, this time with a tone of finality.

"Then the pact is made."

A surge of power exploded through her, a rush of energy so overwhelming that Elara stumbled back, nearly falling to the ground. She felt it—inside her, around her, a force unlike anything she had ever known. The power of the ancient bloodline, the blood of the Bloodborn, was now hers to command.

But at what cost? The shadows that had been her ally were no longer just whispers. They were real. And they would demand their price.

As the chamber returned to stillness, Elara stood there, trembling not from fear, but from the weight of what she had just unleashed. She had made her choice. And now, the ancient rites had bound her to the darkness forever.

As the ritual's power began to ebb, Elara stood in the stillness, her breath coming in shallow gasps. The flickering flames of the torches slowly returned to their normal, steady glow, casting long shadows on the walls. But the shadows were no longer just shapes. They were now a part of her, entwined with the very essence of her being. She could feel their presence lingering, waiting.

For a moment, the room seemed to hold its breath, as if the world itself were waiting to see what would happen next. The air was thick with the weight of the pact she had just made. Every inch of her skin tingled, the remnants of the ritual still vibrating in her veins.

But despite the overwhelming power that coursed through her, there was a gnawing unease, a feeling that something was wrong. It was as if the shadows themselves had been awakened in a way that went beyond her control. She had summoned them, yes, but now they whispered their own desires, their own hunger.

A voice, not the one from the shadows, but something deeper, darker, slithered inside her mind. "You cannot escape what you have bound yourself to. You are ours now, Queen."

The words sent a shiver down her spine, but Elara forced herself to stand tall. She was the Queen, the ruler of the kingdom, and she had not made this choice lightly. She would not allow fear to take root.

"You will not control me," she whispered to the voice inside her head, her words resolute. "I control you."

The laughter that echoed in the depths of her mind was chilling, the sound of something ancient, something old beyond comprehension. "Foolish girl. You think you can control us? The power you seek will consume you in time. We will feed on your strength until there is nothing left of you but a hollow shell."

Elara's hands tightened into fists, the chalice still clutched in her grip. The blood that had spilled into it had long since dried, but she could still feel its power, still taste the sacrifice. She had done this to save her kingdom, to protect her people, and she would not let it be in vain. Not now, when the darkness had already begun to spread.

The door to the chamber creaked open, a sound that cut through the tense silence like a knife. Elara's head snapped toward it, her senses on high alert. She had expected no one, but the figure that entered was one she recognized immediately.

It was Kaelen, her most trusted ally, the general who had fought at her side in countless battles. His armor, once pristine, was now battered and worn from the war that was tearing the kingdom apart. His expression was grim, his eyes shadowed with something that Elara couldn't quite place.

"Elara," he said, his voice hoarse. "I felt it. The ritual… it's done, isn't it?"

She nodded, her gaze still fixed on him, though her mind was racing. Kaelen was no fool; he knew the weight of the power she had just invoked. He could sense it, feel it in the air, like a storm brewing on the horizon.

"Is it everything you hoped for?" he asked, his voice tinged with concern. "Do you feel… different?"

Elara opened her mouth to speak but found herself hesitating. How could she explain it? How could she put into words the swirling chaos inside her, the way the shadows pressed against her, pulling at the very fabric of her soul? She could feel them now, not just as whispers, but as an almost tangible presence within her. They were alive, breathing, waiting.

"I'm stronger," she said finally, though the words felt hollow in her mouth. "But I'm also… not the same."

Kaelen stepped closer, his eyes scanning her face, as if trying to see beyond the façade she had carefully constructed. He reached out a hand, his fingers brushing against her arm, and for a moment, Elara felt the flicker of something—concern, perhaps, or even fear. He was afraid for her.

"You're the Queen, Elara," he said quietly, his voice filled with a depth of emotion she had never heard before. "But don't forget who you are, who you've always been. Don't let the shadows take you."

The words struck her like a blow, and for the first time, she realized just how dangerous this path could be. She had thought that she could wield the power of the ancient rites with precision, that she could control the darkness, but now, with Kaelen's words echoing in her mind, she understood that the price of this power might be higher than she was willing to pay.

The shadows in her mind stirred, a soft hiss of anticipation. "He's right," they whispered, their voices seductive. "You are ours, Queen. You belong to us now."

Elara's hand clenched around the chalice once more, her nails digging into her palm. She had made her choice. She had offered her soul, and in return, she had received power beyond her wildest imagination. But now, the true test had begun. She would have to walk a dangerous path, one where every step forward would bring her closer to the edge of madness.

With a final glance at Kaelen, Elara took a deep breath. "I will not let it consume me," she said, her voice stronger than she felt. "I will control it."

But deep inside, she wondered if that was truly possible.

○ Secrets Unveiled

The room was dimly lit, the shadows of the old castle stretching long across the walls as the wind howled outside, rattling the thick wooden windows. In the center of the chamber, a large stone table stood, covered in ancient scrolls, maps, and relics—each piece a clue, a piece of the puzzle that had eluded the kingdom for centuries. Rhiannon, the High Witch of the North, stood over the table, her fingers tracing the surface of a weathered parchment as she muttered to herself.

Elara, the Queen of the Bloodborn, stepped into the room, her footsteps barely audible on the cold stone floor. Her eyes were weary, her face a mask of determination, yet beneath that mask, there was a flicker of something darker. The weight of the prophecy had never been heavier, the burden of her bloodline pulling at her with every passing day. The whispers of her ancestors, the ancient curse that bound her to the throne, had only grown louder in recent weeks. It was as though the very air around her was thick with the scent of impending doom.

"Rhiannon," Elara's voice was low, tinged with both command and curiosity. "What have you found?"

The witch did not look up. Her fingers continued to move, tracing symbols on the scroll with such precision that it seemed as if she was drawing out a map from the ether itself. After a long pause, she spoke, her voice distant, almost as though she were speaking to herself.

"The curse," Rhiannon began, finally lifting her gaze to meet Elara's. "It's more than just a shadow over your bloodline. It's a chain, Elara, one that binds not just your ancestors, but all those who came before them—each queen, each ruler, cursed to make the same choices. Choices that lead to the same end."

Elara's breath caught in her throat. She had known this truth, buried deep in her soul, but hearing it spoken aloud made it real. The weight of her lineage was not just a metaphor—it was a physical, almost tangible presence that hung over her like a dark cloud. The lives of those who had ruled before her, the lives of those who would come after, were all part of this same terrible cycle.

"You are not just a ruler," Rhiannon continued, her eyes narrowing as she scanned the ancient texts. "You are the key. Your blood is the gateway to breaking the cycle, but it's also what keeps it alive. The prophecy speaks of a queen who will either save the kingdom or bring about its final destruction. The choice has always been yours, but you cannot escape the cost. The cost is your soul."

Elara felt the ground beneath her feet shift, as though the very foundations of her kingdom were crumbling. Her mind raced, the weight of Rhiannon's words pressing down on her chest. Could she truly break the curse? Could she rewrite the fate that had been dictated by blood and magic for so long?

But even as doubt whispered in her mind, something else stirred—an undeniable hunger. The hunger for power. For control. For the chance to finally put an end to the forces that had controlled her for so long.

"I don't fear the cost," Elara said, her voice unwavering, though her heart was a storm of conflicting emotions. "I will face it, no matter what it takes."

Rhiannon's eyes softened, a brief flicker of sadness passing through them. "It's not the cost you should fear, Elara. It's what comes after."

Elara's gaze hardened. She had always known that the throne demanded sacrifices, but now, the true price was becoming clear. The question was no longer whether she would pay it—but how. The witch's words echoed in her mind as she turned to leave the room, her mind already racing ahead, plotting the path to the final confrontation.

Outside, the storm continued to rage, but inside the castle, a quiet resolve settled over Elara. She would no longer be a pawn in the hands of fate. She would choose her destiny, no matter the cost. The secrets of her bloodline were no longer hidden. They had been unveiled, and with them, the truth of her reign. Now, it was up to her to decide whether to rise—or fall.

Elara walked briskly down the long corridor, her boots echoing in the silence. The weight of Rhiannon's words clung to her like a shroud. She had always known that the throne came with its sacrifices, but now, the magnitude of the choice before her was becoming painfully clear. There was no turning back. The kingdom had already begun to suffer under the strain of her indecision, and every moment of hesitation seemed to push her closer to the edge of ruin.

As she reached the door to her private chambers, she stopped for a moment, her hand resting on the cold metal. She could feel the pulse of the kingdom outside, a distant but ever-present hum beneath her skin. The people, the nobles, the warriors—they all looked to her for guidance, for strength. They believed she was the one to lead them out of the darkness, but Elara knew better. Leadership was a fragile illusion, one that could break in an instant.

With a slow exhale, she pushed the door open, stepping into her chamber. Her eyes instinctively went to the large mirror hanging on the far wall. The reflection that stared back at her was not the woman she had hoped to see—the confident queen, poised and untouchable. No, the woman in the mirror was someone else entirely: a woman who had inherited a burden too great to bear, a woman trapped between duty and destiny.

She crossed the room, her fingers brushing the cool glass. For a moment, she saw the faces of the queens who had come before her. They were all there, their eyes filled with the same mix of pride and sorrow. Each had ruled with an iron fist, each had faced the same trials, and each had fallen, one way or another, to the same curse. The bloodline of the Bloodborn had always been a cycle of power and destruction, a never-ending wheel that turned on the bodies of those who dared to wear the crown.

A sharp knock on the door interrupted her thoughts. She turned, her heart quickening, knowing who it was even before the figure stepped into the room.

"Your Majesty," the voice of Captain Thorne came, firm and respectful. "The council awaits your presence. They demand answers."

Elara straightened, turning from the mirror. Her expression was unreadable as she faced the captain, his sharp features betraying no emotion. Thorne had always been a loyal soldier, but loyalty was a double-edged sword. She knew that beneath his calm exterior, he too was conflicted. The kingdom was falling apart, and every decision she made pushed them closer to the brink.

"I will be there shortly," Elara replied, her voice steady. "Tell them to wait."

Thorne hesitated for a moment, his eyes searching hers, before nodding and exiting the room. Elara let out a long breath, feeling the weight of her responsibilities settle back onto her shoulders. She had known that the council would be growing impatient. They could sense the growing unrest within the kingdom. Whispers of rebellion, of fractured loyalties, were beginning to take root. The nobles, once her most trusted allies, were now eyeing each other with distrust. The Bloodborn legacy, once a symbol of power and unity, was now a source of division and fear.

Elara stood motionless for a moment, gathering her thoughts. There was only one path forward. She had to make a choice—one that would either destroy her or set her free.

With a final glance at the mirror, she turned and left the room, her steps steady and purposeful. As she made her way through the castle corridors, the whispers of her ancestors seemed to follow her, their voices urging her forward. The kingdom was on the edge of a precipice, and Elara was the only one who could decide whether they would fall or rise.

When she reached the council chamber, the tension in the air was palpable. The nobles were gathered around the long stone table, their faces a mixture of fear and impatience. At the head of the table sat Lord Gavriel, the leader of the council, his eyes sharp and calculating. His loyalty was questionable, and Elara knew that his allegiance could shift at any moment.

"Your Majesty," Gavriel said with a forced smile as she entered, "We were beginning to wonder if you had forgotten your duty."

Elara's gaze hardened, her voice cutting through the tension like a blade. "I have not forgotten my duty. But I will not be rushed into making a decision that will determine the future of this kingdom."

The room fell silent. The nobles exchanged uneasy glances, but no one dared to speak.

"I know you all fear what lies ahead," Elara continued, her voice unwavering. "But understand this: I will not allow this kingdom to fall into chaos. I will make the necessary sacrifices, no matter the cost."

There was a murmur among the council members, some nodding in agreement, others remaining silent. Lord Gavriel's eyes narrowed, but he said nothing.

"You all know the prophecy," Elara added, her voice growing colder. "I will either break the cycle of blood and death—or I will become the final queen in this cursed lineage. The choice is mine."

As she finished, the tension in the room was almost unbearable. The weight of her words hung heavy in the air. There would be no turning back. The secret that had been unveiled—the truth of her bloodline, the curse that bound her—was now known to all.

The council was silent, awaiting her next move.

3. Into the Abyss

- The Journey to the Forbidden Lands

The air grew thick with anticipation as Elara stood on the precipice, staring out at the unknown expanse before her. The Forbidden Lands—ancient and cursed, a place where no living soul dared to tread. The whispers of her ancestors haunted the winds, warning of the horrors that lay within. Yet, there was no turning back now. She had come too far, and the weight of her destiny pressed down upon her like the very mountains surrounding her.

Her companions, a band of misfit allies she had gathered along the way, stood behind her, their faces etched with the same mix of fear and resolve. Among them was Rhiannon, the enigmatic witch whose magic was as much a curse as it was a blessing, and Varian, a seasoned warrior whose loyalty to Elara had been tested countless times. There were others—strangers united by a common goal, but it was Elara who carried the burden of this journey. She had to find the truth. She had to unlock the power that was hidden in these forsaken lands.

The map that Rhiannon had deciphered led them here, to the edge of the world. It was said that the Forbidden Lands were once the heart of the empire, a thriving kingdom before greed and ambition corrupted it. The gods themselves had forsaken this place, and those who had stayed too long were driven mad by the dark forces that lingered in the shadows. But Elara had no choice. She needed to uncover the ancient artifact that was said to hold the key to defeating the dark power rising in the kingdom. Only here, in the forgotten depths of the land, would she find what she sought.

As they crossed into the wilderness, the air seemed to change. The world around them grew silent, as though the land itself held its breath, watching them with unseen eyes. The forest, twisted and gnarled, seemed to close in on them. Vines with sharp, thorn-like barbs hung from the trees, and the ground was littered with bones—remnants of those who had ventured here before and never returned. The path was treacherous, and every step felt like it could be their last. Yet, Elara pressed forward, her resolve unshaken.

Days passed in a blur of exhaustion and unease. They had to rely on the map and Rhiannon's magic to guide them, for the land seemed intent on confusing them at every turn. The deeper they ventured, the more oppressive the atmosphere became. The sun barely broke through the dense canopy above, casting everything in a perpetual twilight. Strange creatures, barely glimpsed in the corners of their vision, moved in the shadows, and the ground seemed to whisper beneath their feet, as though the land itself had a voice.

One night, as they camped near a dark, stagnant pool, Elara felt a shiver run down her spine. The hairs on the back of her neck stood on end, and the silence was broken only by the distant howls of something unseen. Rhiannon, who had been unusually quiet, seemed to sense the same thing. Her eyes flickered to the horizon, her brow furrowed in concentration. "We are not alone," she murmured, her voice barely a whisper. "Something watches us."

Varian, ever the pragmatist, drew his sword and scanned the surrounding darkness. "We've been followed since we entered the forest. Keep your wits about you."

Elara nodded but didn't speak. The journey had taken a toll on her, and the weight of the choices she had made pressed heavily on her heart. She had no doubt that the forces they sought to escape were closing in on them. She had known from the start that this journey would cost her—perhaps everything—but the fate of the kingdom rested in her hands. There could be no turning back.

The next day, they continued their march through the oppressive wilderness, each step feeling heavier than the last. The Forbidden Lands were a labyrinth, twisting and changing, a place where the laws of nature seemed to warp and bend. But with each trial, each struggle, Elara felt herself growing stronger. The power that flowed through her veins—ancient and untapped—stirred with a hunger of its own, responding to the land that had been abandoned by time and gods. It was as if the very essence of the earth was calling to her, beckoning her toward something greater than herself.

As they neared the heart of the Forbidden Lands, the air grew colder, and the trees seemed to bend toward them, their twisted branches clawing at the sky. It was then that Elara saw it—an ancient temple, half-buried in the earth, its black stone walls covered in cryptic runes that pulsed with an eerie light. The artifact she sought was within. But so, too, was the darkness that had been waiting for her, for it had always been there, hidden in the shadows, waiting for the right moment to strike.

They had reached their destination, but their true journey was only just beginning.

The temple loomed before them, its presence both unsettling and magnificent. The stone walls, slick with an unnatural sheen, seemed to pulse with life, their runes glowing faintly in the dim light that filtered through the twisted canopy above. The air was thick with the scent of decay, as if time had long since forgotten this place. Yet, there was something undeniably powerful about it. Elara could feel it—the pull, the call of something ancient and forbidden.

Rhiannon stepped forward, her fingers tracing the air as though weaving a spell to shield them from whatever malevolent force lay beyond the threshold. "This place is old," she murmured, her voice filled with a mixture of awe and caution. "Older than the empire itself. We must tread carefully."

Varian shifted uneasily beside Elara, his grip tightening on the hilt of his sword. "The deeper we go, the more I feel like we're being drawn into something we can't control."

Elara didn't respond, her gaze fixed on the entrance. The temple beckoned her, the weight of its history and power pressing down on her shoulders. She had no time for fear or hesitation. The kingdom, her people, and the lives of those she loved depended on what lay within. The artifact—whatever it was—had to be found, no matter the cost.

With a final, resolute breath, she stepped forward, crossing the threshold into the darkness. The others followed, but the moment they entered, the temperature seemed to drop, and an oppressive silence descended. It was as though the temple was holding its breath, waiting for them to make the next move.

The walls were adorned with ancient carvings, depicting scenes of gods and creatures long forgotten. Some of the figures seemed to watch them, their eyes gleaming with a strange, unsettling awareness. Elara's footsteps echoed in the vast emptiness, each one resonating like a distant drumbeat, reminding her of the enormity of the task ahead.

They moved deeper into the temple, winding through narrow corridors and vast, open chambers filled with shadows that seemed to stretch unnaturally long. The air was thick with dust, and the floor was littered with remnants of a long-dead civilization—broken statues, shattered relics, and ancient scrolls, their contents lost to time. It was as though the temple had once been a place of power and worship, now abandoned and forgotten, swallowed by the very darkness it had once tried to contain.

At the heart of the temple, they found a large, circular chamber, its walls lined with more runes that glowed faintly in the darkness. At the center of the room stood a pedestal, upon which rested an object covered by a dark cloth. Elara's pulse quickened, her every instinct telling her that this was it—the artifact she had been searching for.

But as she stepped forward to claim it, something shifted. A low, guttural growl echoed through the chamber, followed by a chilling screech that sent a shiver down Elara's spine. From the shadows, figures began to emerge—creatures twisted and deformed, their bodies contorted in unnatural ways, their eyes glowing with malevolent intent.

Elara drew her sword, the familiar weight of it comforting in her hand, but she knew it would not be enough. These were not mere beasts to be slain. They were something darker, something older.

"We're not alone," Rhiannon whispered, her voice strained. "They've been waiting for us."

Varian stepped forward, his stance wide, ready for battle. "We fight together," he said, his voice unwavering. "We're not leaving without that artifact."

Elara nodded, her eyes locked on the creatures that surrounded them. The air seemed to thicken, the oppressive atmosphere closing in as the shadows took form. The creatures hissed, their movements jerky and erratic, as if they were both part of the temple and separate from it—born of the darkness, yet tied to the very heart of the land.

Without warning, the creatures lunged, their jagged claws slashing through the air. Elara moved swiftly, parrying the first strike with her sword. The battle erupted around them, the clashing of steel and the hiss of magic filling the air. Rhiannon's spells crackled with energy, creating barriers of light that held the creatures at bay, but they were relentless.

For every blow they landed, another creature seemed to rise from the shadows, more ferocious than the last. Elara's heart pounded in her chest as she fought with every ounce of strength she had, her focus solely on the pedestal and the artifact that lay just beyond reach.

She had to get to it.

A moment of clarity washed over her, and Elara broke from the fray, her legs carrying her toward the pedestal. She could feel the power pulsing in the air, the ancient magic that surged through the temple and called to her. She reached out, her fingers brushing the dark cloth that covered the artifact.

But as she touched it, a wave of energy blasted through the chamber, throwing her backward with a force that stole the breath from her lungs. She hit the ground hard, her vision blurred and her body aching from the impact. The creatures roared in fury, but they did not approach the pedestal. Something held them back—something that Elara could not yet comprehend.

Rhiannon's voice broke through the chaos, her words laced with urgency. "Elara, you've triggered something. The temple is reacting to you!"

Elara pushed herself to her feet, her mind racing. The artifact had reacted to her touch, but not in the way she had expected. The temple was alive, and it would not let her claim its prize so easily. The creatures were only the beginning. The true challenge was yet to come.

As she rose to face the darkness again, Elara realized that she had only just begun to understand the true power of the Forbidden Lands. And with it came a terrifying truth: not all forces were meant to be controlled. Some, like the artifact, had their own will, and it was that will that would determine the fate of everything—and everyone—in its path.

- Trials of the Forgotten Ones

The journey into the Forbidden Lands was never one to be taken lightly. It was a path that had been abandoned by many over the centuries, a place where even the bravest warriors and wisest scholars had once dared to venture, only to return broken or not at all. Elara knew this, and yet, here she was, leading the charge into the abyss that awaited her and her companions. The air was thick with the weight of ancient secrets, and the ground beneath their feet seemed to pulse with an energy that had been dormant for far too long.

As they ventured deeper into the heart of the Forgotten Lands, the once lush and vibrant landscape gave way to a desolate wasteland, scarred by time and war. The sky above was dark, as though the sun itself feared to shine on this forsaken place. Jagged mountains loomed in the distance, their peaks lost in the swirling fog that clung to them like a shroud. There was no sound here, not even the whisper of wind or the chirping of birds. It was as if the land itself had been silenced by some dark force.

Elara's footsteps were heavy, each one resonating with the weight of responsibility that rested on her shoulders. She had not come here for glory or honor. She had come for answers—answers to the questions that had haunted her since the moment she had inherited the throne. What was the true nature of the bloodline she carried? What dark forces lay in wait, and what did they want from her?

The others in her group were just as apprehensive, though they did their best to hide it. Rhiannon, the fierce and enigmatic witch, walked beside her, her eyes scanning the surroundings with a wariness that spoke volumes. She was the only one who seemed to understand the gravity of the journey. The rest of the group—Kai, the young and idealistic knight, and Aric, the once proud soldier turned rogue—followed silently, their thoughts their own.

They had all been chosen for this mission, but none of them fully understood the trials they would face. They were not just walking into a dangerous land; they were walking into a trial of their very souls. The Forgotten Ones, as the ancients had called them, were said to test all who dared to enter their domain, and the trials were not of the body, but of the mind and spirit.

As they crossed a barren valley, a cold wind suddenly swept across them, carrying with it the faintest whisper—voices, perhaps, or something more. Elara paused, her heart quickening. The sound was distant, but it was enough to send a chill down her spine. Rhiannon stiffened beside her, her hand moving instinctively to the dark amulet that hung from her neck.

"They're near," Rhiannon whispered, her voice barely audible above the wind. "The Forgotten Ones."

Elara nodded, steeling herself for what lay ahead. She knew that the trials would be unlike anything she had ever faced before. The Forgotten Ones were not mere monsters or demons; they were ancient beings, the remnants of a time long past. They were the guardians of secrets, of knowledge, and of power, and they would not give up their treasures without a fight.

As they continued, the landscape grew darker still. The trees, once full of life, now stood as twisted, blackened skeletons, their branches reaching out like gnarled hands. The ground was uneven, marked with cracks that seemed to breathe, exhaling a foul-smelling mist. The path ahead was shrouded in shadows, and Elara could feel the oppressive weight of the place pressing down on her.

Then, as if in answer to the silence, a figure emerged from the shadows. It was tall and cloaked, its face hidden beneath the hood, but Elara could feel its gaze, cold and all-knowing. The figure raised its hand, and a deep, resonant voice filled the air.

"You have come to face the trials," it intoned. "But are you ready to confront the truth of who you are? The blood that runs through your veins, the power that you seek—will it destroy you, or will it make you stronger?"

Elara's heart skipped a beat. She had known this moment would come, but the weight of the words still hit her with a force she was not prepared for.

"I am ready," she said, her voice steady despite the fear gnawing at her insides. She had no choice but to be ready. This was the only way forward.

The figure nodded, and with a slow, deliberate motion, it stepped aside, revealing the path that lay ahead.

"The trials begin now," it said, its voice fading into the stillness. "Only those who are truly worthy will survive."

With that, Elara and her companions stepped forward into the unknown, the trials of the Forgotten Ones beginning in earnest. They would face tests of strength, courage, and perhaps most of all, their deepest fears. But Elara knew one thing for certain: there was no turning back now. The fate of her kingdom, and her very soul, depended on what lay ahead.

As the group continued down the path, the silence became unbearable. Each step felt heavier, as though the land itself was pushing against them, unwilling to let them pass. The air thickened, becoming harder to breathe, and the temperature seemed to drop with each passing moment. Elara pulled her cloak tighter around her, but it did little to fend off the growing chill.

Rhiannon's pace slowed slightly, her dark eyes flicking from side to side. Her senses, honed by years of training in the arcane, were alert to the subtle disturbances in the air—the magic that lay dormant, waiting to be unleashed. "We are not alone," she muttered, her voice strained. "I can feel their eyes upon us."

Elara nodded grimly, though she didn't speak. She, too, could sense something—something ancient and malevolent, just beyond the edge of her perception. The trials of the Forgotten Ones were not merely tests of physical endurance. They were a trial of the mind, the spirit, and the soul. Each of them would face not only their greatest fears, but also the temptations that might break their resolve.

Suddenly, the ground before them cracked open, splitting with an ominous roar. A dense fog poured out from the rift, swallowing the landscape in its murky depths. It was thick and suffocating, the smell of decay and rot clinging to the air. From within the fog, whispers rose—a cacophony of voices, too many to count. Some sounded familiar, others strange, and some seemed to echo from deep within Elara's own mind.

A voice, cold and insistent, rang out above the others, "Step forward, Elara."

She froze. The voice was not Rhiannon's or any of the others'. It was a voice she had not heard in years—a voice she had hoped to forget. It was the voice of her mother.

"Elara... why do you hesitate?" The voice was gentle, coaxing, yet laden with an undercurrent of something darker, something far more sinister. "You've always known your destiny. You were born to rule. To lead. To be more than you are now."

The fog parted slightly, revealing a figure in the distance. It was a woman—tall, regal, and draped in flowing robes of crimson. Her features were soft, almost ethereal, yet Elara could see the sharpness in her eyes, the calculating look that had once filled her mother's gaze.

"Come to me, child," the voice called again, this time filled with an undeniable command. "You need only accept what is yours. All you need to do is take my hand, and all will be as it was meant to be."

Elara's heart pounded in her chest. For a moment, she was paralyzed. The weight of the past, the memories of her mother's manipulation and the power she had wielded, threatened to overwhelm her. Her mother had been a queen—a tyrant, yes, but one with vision, strength, and cunning. The offer to claim that power, to become the ruler she had always been groomed to be, was tempting.

But Elara had learned through pain and betrayal that power came at a cost. She had seen the damage her mother's rule had done to her people, to her family. It was not a path she wanted to walk again.

Rhiannon's voice broke through her thoughts, sharp and urgent. "Elara, do not listen to it. This is a trick, a test. You know better than this."

With a forceful shake of her head, Elara tore her gaze away from the figure in the mist. She turned toward her companions, their faces strained with fear and determination. She could see the same conflict in their eyes, the same temptation to take the easy way, to claim the power that had been promised to them. But none of them were born to lead as her mother had, and none of them would fall for such tricks.

The figure in the mist dissipated, and the voice fell silent. The fog began to lift, and with it, the oppressive atmosphere that had surrounded them. They had passed the first trial.

"Do not think that was the only one," Rhiannon warned. "This place will show us things we wish we never knew. We must remain strong."

Elara nodded, though the lingering echo of her mother's voice still haunted her. The trial was only beginning, and the real tests awaited.

They moved forward, the rift closing behind them as they pressed deeper into the Forgotten Lands. The further they went, the more the land seemed to warp and twist, as though it were alive, watching them with a malicious intent. Shadows seemed to stretch unnaturally, curling and reaching out like fingers, while strange, shimmering lights flickered in the corners of their vision.

They didn't speak as they moved, the silence stretching longer between them with each step. The path grew narrower, the trees more twisted, their branches reaching out like skeletal hands. It felt as though they were being funneled toward something—a destination they were not yet ready to face.

Ahead, the air grew thick with a tangible sense of dread. The earth beneath their feet shifted again, as though the ground itself was breathing, waiting. And then, as they neared the edge of a cliff, a sharp, sudden roar split the silence.

A massive, monstrous shape emerged from the shadows, a hulking beast with eyes like burning coals. Its body was covered in scales, and its claws gleamed like obsidian. It towered over them, its wings stretching wide, casting a shadow that seemed to consume the light. The Forgotten Ones had sent their first trial—one of physical might.

The creature snarled, its breath hot and foul, filling the air with the stench of death. Elara's heart raced as the beast lowered its head, fixing its gaze on her. It was clear that it was her challenge, her trial to face.

"Fight or fall," it growled, the words vibrating through the ground.

With a deep breath, Elara gripped her sword tightly. This was only the beginning. The Forgotten Ones were not finished with her yet. The true test of her strength, will, and resolve was only just beginning.

- The Depths of Despair

The cold wind whipped through the desolate landscape, carrying with it an eerie silence that seemed to press against the very soul. Elara stood at the edge of the abyss, the chasm before her yawning deep into the earth. There was no light here—only shadows that stretched long and unyielding, as if the darkness itself was alive, hungry for something more. She took a breath, trying to steady herself, but the air felt thick, as if the very atmosphere was laced with despair.

Behind her, the remnants of her once-proud army followed in silence, their faces ashen, their spirits broken. The battle they had fought was over, and it had been a crushing defeat. Vanguard had struck harder than expected, and the forces of the old world seemed to be swarming from every corner, eager to tear down everything she had worked for. The blood in her veins ran cold, the weight of what was ahead pressing down on her like a crushing weight.

As the wind howled around them, Rhiannon, the witch of the forgotten lands, approached Elara cautiously, her dark eyes gleaming with an unsettling mixture of concern and something else—perhaps a deep knowing of the darkness that lay ahead. She was the only one who truly understood the depths they had descended into. The ancient magics that bound their fates together were frail now, straining under the pressure of betrayal, loss, and the looming destruction of everything they had once held dear.

"Elara," Rhiannon spoke, her voice low, barely above a whisper, as if speaking too loudly might shatter the fragile barrier between them and whatever lay beyond. "This path... it leads to more than just death. It leads to the very heart of the curse."

Elara turned to face her, eyes narrowing. "I know what it leads to. And I know what must be done."

But even as she spoke those words, doubt gnawed at her. Was she truly prepared to face what awaited in the depths? To confront the very power that had cursed her bloodline for centuries? She had always known the prophecy, had always felt the burden of the blood in her veins. But now, standing at the precipice, the reality of it all felt like an unshakable weight.

Rhiannon's gaze softened, but there was little comfort to be found in it. "There is no turning back once you step inside," she cautioned. "The spirits that dwell in these depths... they will test you. They will make you confront everything you've ever feared. And some things are better left buried, Elara."

But the queen's resolve was unshakable. She had no choice. If she was to reclaim her kingdom, to defeat Vanguard and end the curse that had haunted her people for so long, she would have to face this. There was no other way.

With a final glance toward her companions, Elara stepped forward, her boots crunching on the dry earth as she descended into the abyss. The air grew colder, the shadows longer, and the silence deeper. It was as if the very earth itself was swallowing her whole.

She didn't know what awaited in the depths, but she had no choice. It was either this—or the end of everything.

As she ventured further into the darkness, the echoes of the past whispered around her, their voices faint but clear, like distant cries of agony. Each step she took seemed to carry her further away from the world she knew, into a place where the very fabric of reality seemed to warp and bend.

This was not a place for the living. And yet, here she was, plunging deeper into its heart, determined to uncover the truth hidden within. The answers she sought lay at the bottom of this dark chasm—answers that would either save her or destroy her.

But even as she moved deeper, there was something more than just the weight of the prophecy pressing down on her. There was a sense of something ancient stirring in the dark, something that had been waiting for this very moment. And as the shadows seemed to shift around her, Elara couldn't shake the feeling that she was being watched.

The Depths of Despair were not merely a place. They were a test—a trial that would determine if Elara was truly worthy of the crown she wore, of the legacy she carried in her blood, or if she would be consumed by the very darkness she had fought so hard to escape.

With each step, the tension mounted, and the air grew heavier. The fear in her chest began to rise, but so did her determination. She would not fail. Not now, not when everything depended on her. She would descend into the heart of darkness, face the horrors that awaited her, and emerge victorious—or not at all. There was no middle ground.

And so, she pressed on, deeper into the abyss.

The deeper Elara descended, the heavier the air became, thick with the weight of centuries of suffering. The blackened walls of the chasm seemed to pulse with a life of their own, their jagged edges reaching out like claws, scraping at the edges of her mind. Each step she took sent an unsettling echo through the hollow void, a reminder that she was not alone here.

In the distance, she could hear a soft whisper—a voice carried on the wind, but it was not the voice of her companions. It was faint, almost indecipherable, but there was a certain rhythm to it, like an ancient chant. Her heartbeat quickened as she instinctively knew that it was no ordinary sound. This was something older, something that had existed long before her birth.

Rhiannon's warnings echoed in her mind: *The spirits that dwell in these depths will test you. They will make you confront everything you've ever feared.*

The whispers grew louder as she advanced, swirling around her, wrapping themselves around her thoughts like vines, seeking to choke the will from her. She had always prided herself on her strength, on her ability to stand tall in the face of any challenge. But now, as the voices pressed in, she felt the first flicker of doubt.

"Who's there?" she called out, her voice trembling despite her best efforts to stay steady. The sound of her own words felt alien in the thick silence of the abyss, swallowed almost immediately by the consuming darkness.

The shadows seemed to shift, as if reacting to her challenge. And then, from the blackness ahead, a figure emerged.

At first, it was nothing more than a silhouette, a shape outlined against the void. But as it drew closer, Elara's breath caught in her throat. The figure was tall, draped in tattered robes that fluttered as if caught in an unseen breeze. Its face was hidden beneath a hood, but there was something unnerving about the way it moved, the way it glided through the shadows without a sound.

"Elara..." The voice was deep, almost too deep, a hollow resonance that sent a chill racing down her spine. The figure stopped in front of her, and its hooded head tilted slightly, as if studying her.

A thousand emotions rushed through her—fear, confusion, anger—but above all, a burning need to understand. "What are you?" she demanded, her voice louder now, trying to steady herself.

The figure remained silent for a moment, as though weighing her words. When it spoke again, its voice was softer, almost sympathetic. "I am what you fear most. I am the reflection of the darkness that lies within you."

Elara's heart skipped a beat. She had always been aware of the curse that ran through her bloodline—the darkness that had followed her every step, the whispers in her mind telling her she was destined to destroy rather than save. But hearing it spoken aloud, feeling the weight of those words settle over her like a shroud, sent a wave of cold terror through her.

"No," she whispered, shaking her head as if to banish the thought. "I will not be that. I refuse to be."

The figure's voice softened further, and for the briefest of moments, Elara could almost hear a trace of sadness in its tone. "You refuse, but can you escape it? Can you outrun the curse that has been woven into the very fabric of your existence? Or will you let it consume you, as it has consumed all who came before you?"

Elara's mind raced. She knew the truth of what it said. The curse had claimed her ancestors, each one falling deeper into the abyss until there was nothing left of them but shadows of their former selves. Would she be any different? Would she be strong enough to defy it?

A surge of defiance rose within her chest. She was Elara Bloodborne, queen of the forsaken lands, and she would not bow to the darkness. She could feel her heart beating in her chest, a rhythm of life and strength that refused to falter.

"No," she said again, this time with more conviction. "I will not allow it. I will control my own fate."

The figure's hood tilted once more, as if considering her words. Then, it began to fade, melting into the shadows like mist dissipating in the dawn.

"You will face much worse before the end," it whispered, the voice fading with it. "This is only the beginning."

The darkness seemed to close in around her once more, but Elara stood firm, her fists clenched at her sides. She would not let the shadows claim her. Not today.

But the path ahead was far from clear. As she moved deeper into the chasm, the whispers continued to haunt her, the voices of the past and the weight of her own fears pressing in from all sides. Every step felt heavier, as though the very earth beneath her feet was trying to drag her down into the abyss.

And yet, despite the crushing pressure, despite the darkness that threatened to swallow her whole, Elara pressed on. She had made her choice. She would not turn back.

The abyss stretched on before her, endless and deep, and she knew that her journey had only just begun. The trials that awaited her in the depths would shape her, test her, and perhaps even break her. But she would face them head-on, as she always had.

For there was no other way.

4. Alliances of Blood

○ The Last Hope

The sun had long set, casting a soft glow over the encampment as Elara sat by the flickering fire. The heat of the flames did little to comfort her; it was the weight of the choices she had made—and the ones she had yet to make—that burdened her heart. Her eyes, still sharp and perceptive, scanned the horizon, watching for any sign of the enemy. It felt like a dream, one that was slipping through her fingers, yet the reality of it all was far more suffocating.

The kingdom she had once ruled with pride and strength now lay in ruins. The familiar faces of those she had trusted were now shadows in the dark, and the land that had once flourished under her reign was now a battleground for survival. She had always known that power came with a price, but nothing could have prepared her for the devastating cost she had to pay. Allies turned traitors, old enemies returned from the grave, and the bloodline she was born into—her legacy—was now tainted with betrayal and secrets long buried.

Yet, in the midst of this overwhelming despair, a flicker of hope remained.

Her hand instinctively moved to the hilt of her sword, the cool metal against her skin offering a momentary sense of security. The blade, forged from the very heart of the kingdom, was not just a weapon—it was a symbol. A symbol of her resolve. A symbol of the blood that had been spilled to protect this land. And now, it was all that stood between her and the darkness that threatened to consume everything she loved.

"Your Majesty," a voice interrupted her thoughts. It was Caelan, her most trusted captain and a man who had stood by her side through the worst of times. His presence, though comforting, only reminded her of the weight of her responsibilities. He had been with her from the beginning, and now, it seemed, he was the last of the loyal ones.

"We've received word," he said, his voice tense but steady. "The Vanguard is on the move. They'll be here by dawn."

Elara's gaze hardened, her eyes narrowing as the flames danced in the night. "We knew this day would come," she murmured. "But now it's upon us."

Caelan took a step closer, lowering his voice. "There's more. The scouts have reported strange movements in the forest beyond. We're not just facing an army—we're facing something darker. Something… older."

Elara's heart skipped a beat. The darkness that had once been a whisper in the back of her mind was now taking form, and it had come for her kingdom. She had heard the legends—the tales of ancient forces that had once ruled the land, long before the bloodline of the kings and queens had risen. But she had never truly believed in them. Until now.

"We can't do this alone," Elara said, the weight of her words sinking into her soul. "The people need hope. A sign that we can win."

She rose to her feet, her movements deliberate. "We must find the last of the ancient alliances. The ones who have been lost to history. They are our only chance. Without them, we will fall."

Caelan nodded, his face grim. "And what of the bloodborne curse? Can we truly trust the power it offers?"

Elara looked down at the blood-red stone she wore around her neck, a reminder of the curse that had been passed down through generations. She had always feared it—its dark magic, its insatiable thirst for power. But now, faced with the reality of their situation, she knew there was no other choice.

"We don't have the luxury of trust," she replied quietly. "We use it. Or we perish."

The camp was quiet for a moment, the only sound the crackling of the fire and the distant howls of wolves. Elara stood there, looking into the flames, her mind racing. She could feel the weight of the kingdom's future pressing on her shoulders. She was the last hope. The last chance for everything she had fought for.

But even as she steeled herself for what lay ahead, doubts lingered. Was it too late? Could they truly defeat the darkness that had taken root in their world? And what price would she have to pay to save her people?

With a deep breath, Elara turned toward Caelan. "Prepare the men. At dawn, we ride. We find the alliances, and we make our stand."

Caelan hesitated for a moment before nodding. "I'll see to it, Your Majesty."

As he walked away, Elara stood alone by the fire, the weight of her decision hanging heavy in the air. She was the last hope. The future of the kingdom rested on her shoulders, and the path ahead was uncertain, fraught with danger and darkness.

But there was no turning back now.

The time for doubt had passed.

The night stretched on, the chill of the air seeping into Elara's bones. She could feel the familiar weight of the crown that had once graced her brow, a symbol of her authority, now resting in the back of her mind like an unwelcome reminder. The kingdom, her kingdom, was slipping away—its ruins scattered like broken memories. And yet, here she stood, the last hope, with no clear path forward but the one that led into the unknown.

The flickering firelight cast shadows that seemed to whisper in the wind, a thousand voices calling from the past, the lives lost, the promises broken. She could hear her father's voice in her mind, his warnings of the ever-present threat of the Vanguard, a power born of shadows and dark magic. But those warnings had always felt distant, stories to be told around a campfire, not warnings for a time such as this. And yet now, with the enemy closing in, the stories felt all too real.

A rustling from behind her broke her reverie. She turned to find Caelan approaching once more, his face tight with the weight of his own thoughts. There was something in his eyes—a flicker of something Elara couldn't quite place. Fear? No, not fear. More like... uncertainty.

"Your Majesty," he began, his voice low, almost hesitant. "We've received word from the scouts. There's a traitor among us."

Elara's heart skipped a beat. A traitor? Here? Among her loyal men?

"Who?" she asked sharply, her voice steady despite the rush of panic that threatened to rise within her.

Caelan hesitated for a moment, then spoke the name that sent a cold shiver down her spine.

"Darian."

Her blood ran cold. Darian had been one of her most trusted commanders, a man whose loyalty had never been questioned. His name had once been synonymous with strength, courage, and honor. He had fought beside her in countless battles, had bled for the kingdom. How could it be him?

"Elara..." Caelan's voice softened as he stepped closer. "I know what you're thinking. But the scouts found evidence—he's been meeting with the Vanguard. He's been feeding them information."

The weight of the words hit Elara like a physical blow. The betrayal felt like a knife to her chest. How could Darian, of all people, betray her? Betray everything they had fought for?

"Are you certain?" she asked, though she already knew the answer. It was written in Caelan's face, in the way his shoulders were tense, like he was bracing for her reaction.

"Yes," Caelan replied, his eyes filled with sorrow. "We found his seal. The same one the Vanguard uses to mark their spies."

Elara took a deep breath, trying to steady herself. The fire crackled behind her, the flames dancing like the flicker of her thoughts. A traitor in their midst. It was a wound she couldn't ignore, but she had no time to mourn. The Vanguard was coming, and Darian's betrayal only deepened the gravity of their situation.

"Where is he now?" Elara asked, her voice colder than the night air.

"Locked in the holding cells," Caelan answered. "We can deal with him in the morning."

She nodded, but the decision gnawed at her insides. What was she supposed to do with him? He was a traitor, yes, but he had been her friend. A man she had trusted with her life. How could she reconcile that?

"Leave him for now," Elara said finally, her tone decisive, though the conflict inside her remained. "We have more pressing matters. The Vanguard is still our main concern."

Caelan bowed slightly. "As you command, Your Majesty."

He turned to leave, but Elara called after him.

"Caelan... If we do not survive this, if everything we have fought for falls, will the blood we've spilled ever mean anything?"

He paused, his back still turned to her. For a long moment, the only sound was the crackling of the fire.

"I do not know," he said quietly, without turning around. "But we have to fight. We have no choice."

Elara watched him disappear into the darkness, his silhouette blending with the night. She knew he was right. They had no choice. There was only one path forward, and it led to war.

The flickering flames reflected in her eyes, and for a moment, she could almost hear the whispers of the past. Her father's warnings. The legends of the ancient powers. The blood that had been spilled to protect this kingdom, and the blood that would soon be spilled again.

But she was ready. The time for hesitation had passed. Tomorrow, they would ride. Tomorrow, they would face the Vanguard.

And tomorrow, the fate of the kingdom would be decided.

With one final glance at the dark horizon, Elara turned and walked into the night, her resolve hardening like steel. The last hope was still alive, and as long as she drew breath, she would fight for it.

- Enemy Within

The cold wind howled through the narrow streets of the kingdom, carrying with it a sense of unease that seemed to settle in the very bones of the people. Whispers of rebellion had begun to stir, but no one knew where the true danger lay. Elara, Queen of the Bloodborn, stood at the balcony of the royal palace, her eyes scanning the horizon as if searching for something she couldn't yet see. Her heart, burdened with the weight of leadership, felt heavier with each passing day.

The betrayal that had been festering within her own court was more dangerous than any external threat. The enemy within was a more insidious force, one that could tear apart everything she had fought to build. She had seen the signs, the subtle shifts in the loyalty of those closest to her. Her trusted advisors, the noble families, the generals of her army—they all had their own agendas, their own ambitions. It was a kingdom divided, and Elara was caught in the center, struggling to hold the fragile threads of power together.

It had begun months ago, in the quiet moments when she thought no one was watching. She had caught fleeting glimpses of her closest allies exchanging glances that spoke volumes—glances that spoke of secrets, of hidden alliances, of plans not yet revealed. Her most trusted general, Aldric, had become distant, his once unshakable loyalty now tinged with something darker. He had started questioning her decisions in private, making subtle suggestions that she could not ignore. He was a man of honor, but even honor could be manipulated when the right words were whispered in the right ears.

Elara turned from the balcony, her fingers tightening around the cold stone as she made her way back inside. She had to act, but with whom could she trust? The court was a web of lies and half-truths, each thread leading somewhere she could not predict. The enemy was not just outside her walls, it was within them—lurking in the shadows, waiting for the right moment to strike.

As she sat in her chambers, her mind raced. She had known that ruling a kingdom would be difficult, but this—this treachery from within—was something she had never been prepared for. She had fought wars, endured sieges, faced death countless times. But the quiet, calculating betrayal of those she had called allies felt like a wound that would never heal.

Her mind drifted to the words of Rhiannon, the mysterious witch who had warned her of a curse that ran through her bloodline. "The blood of your ancestors is both your strength and your weakness," she had said. "The enemy within will rise when the time is right. Trust no one, Elara." At the time, Elara had dismissed the warning as superstition. But now, as she faced the threat within her own walls, those words echoed in her mind, too chilling to ignore.

The next morning, Elara summoned Aldric to her private chamber. The tension between them was palpable, the air thick with unspoken words. He entered with his usual confidence, but Elara could see the shift in his demeanor—he was hiding something. Her gaze narrowed as she met his eyes.

"Aldric," she said, her voice steady but cold. "We need to talk."

He stiffened but nodded, closing the door behind him. "Of course, Your Majesty."

"Tell me the truth," Elara began, her voice cutting through the silence. "What is it that you are planning behind my back? Who do you serve now, Aldric? Is it me? Or is it someone else?"

His face remained impassive, but she could see the flicker of something in his eyes—something akin to regret. He opened his mouth to speak, but the words never came. Instead, he turned away, pacing to the far side of the room, as if the very confrontation had unsettled him. Elara waited, her gaze unwavering.

After a long pause, he finally spoke, his voice low. "There are forces at work that you don't understand, Elara. Forces you cannot control. I...I didn't want this. I never wanted to betray you."

The words hit her like a punch to the gut. Betrayal. It had always been a distant possibility, something she had prepared herself for, but hearing it from Aldric's lips made it real. The enemy within. The one she had trusted above all others.

"Then who do you serve?" Elara's voice was barely a whisper, but it carried the weight of a thousand fears.

Aldric turned to face her, his expression now one of shame. "There are those who would see you fall, Elara. Those who believe your bloodline is a curse, not a gift. They are using me, and I—" His voice faltered, but he quickly regained his composure. "I'm sorry. I never meant for it to go this far. I thought I could protect you from the truth, but the truth is far more dangerous than I ever imagined."

Elara's heart pounded in her chest, her breath shallow. She had always known there were enemies outside her kingdom, but now she realized the most dangerous ones were the ones who had been closest to her all along.

"You are not the only one who is trapped by forces beyond your control, Aldric," Elara said, her voice a mixture of sadness and determination. "But now we have a choice. We can either fight this together, or you can leave and let them win."

For the first time in months, Aldric's gaze softened. He stepped forward, his hand outstretched, as if offering her a lifeline. "I will stand by you, Your Majesty. I swear it. We will fight this, together."

The enemy within had revealed itself, but this was not the end. It was only the beginning. Elara knew that the road ahead would be fraught with peril, but with Aldric's help, perhaps she could navigate the treacherous waters of betrayal and emerge stronger than before.

As the sun set over the kingdom, Elara made a vow to herself and to the people she ruled: the enemy within would not destroy her. She would fight back, no matter the cost. The reckoning was coming, and she would be ready.

The following days passed in a haze of tension and uncertainty. Elara, still reeling from the revelation of Aldric's involvement with the conspirators, had no choice but to remain vigilant. She could not allow the treachery within her walls to tear apart the fragile unity she had worked so hard to build. Every moment felt like a carefully orchestrated dance, where one misstep could spell disaster.

Aldric, though repentant, remained distant, as if the weight of his actions had become too much to bear. He had pledged his loyalty to her once more, but Elara knew that trust could never be so easily rebuilt. The cracks in their relationship were too deep, the shadows of doubt lingering in every conversation. She could feel his eyes on her, a silent plea for forgiveness that she could not yet grant.

With each passing day, the whispers of rebellion grew louder, carried on the wind and into the ears of every noble and commoner alike. The enemy was no longer hidden in the shadows—they were bold, moving with a confidence that made Elara's stomach churn. She had learned long ago that power was rarely maintained through kindness alone; it was forged in blood and steel. But even so, the thought of turning against her own people was something she could not stomach. The lines between loyalty and betrayal had blurred beyond recognition.

Elara sought solace in the ancient texts of the Bloodborn—a sacred lineage that had ruled for generations. She poured over the scrolls, seeking any clue, any prophecy that might shed light on her path. The warnings from Rhiannon echoed in her mind, the cryptic words resonating with a deeper sense of foreboding. The enemy within, she realized, was not just Aldric or the conspirators within the court. It was a curse that had been passed down through the bloodline of her ancestors. The Bloodborn were both rulers and outcasts, bound by a destiny that no one could escape.

On the seventh night after their conversation, Elara called for a secret meeting with her most trusted remaining advisors. She needed to plan her next move, to ensure that the traitors in her midst were rooted out before their plans could come to fruition. The room was dimly lit, the shadows dancing along the walls as her closest allies gathered in silence. Aldric stood at the far end of the table, his eyes lowered, unwilling to meet her gaze. He had been summoned, but his presence was a silent reminder of the trust he had nearly shattered.

"Thank you for coming," Elara began, her voice calm but firm. "There is no time to waste. The enemy has already begun to move. We must act swiftly to prevent further damage."

The room was filled with a quiet tension, each person acutely aware of the stakes at hand. Elara's most trusted strategist, Lord Aric, leaned forward, his sharp eyes never leaving her face.

"We know the rebels are gathering in the eastern provinces," he said, his voice a low rumble. "But there are more dangerous elements within the court. We must focus on them first. It is no longer just about keeping the kingdom intact—it is about preserving your reign, Your Majesty."

Elara nodded slowly, her fingers tracing the edge of the map spread across the table. The ink had faded over the years, but the shape of the kingdom remained the same, a constant reminder of what was at stake. The rebels were a threat, yes, but it was the traitors within her own walls that worried her the most.

"I agree," Elara replied. "But we cannot move too openly. We cannot risk alerting them to our plans. We must find who is pulling the strings behind the scenes, who is feeding them information."

Aldric shifted uncomfortably but remained silent, his guilt hanging over him like a shadow. Elara noticed the way his jaw clenched as he tried to suppress the turmoil within him. She was torn between her desire for justice and the loyalty that had once bound them together. But there was no room for sentimentality now. The future of the kingdom depended on swift and decisive action.

"I have a few suspects," Lord Aric continued, his voice cold. "There are a number of nobles who have been growing restless, questioning your decisions in private. They've been seen meeting in the dead of night. I believe they are already in communication with the rebels. But finding solid proof has been... difficult."

Elara's eyes narrowed as she processed the information. The rebellion was not just a random gathering of dissatisfied subjects; it was a well-coordinated effort, one that had been months in the making. And if her suspicions were correct, the rebellion had the support of some of the most influential families in the kingdom.

"We must act quickly," Elara said, her voice hardening with resolve. "We need to root out the traitors before they can move against us. But we must be careful. I want no bloodshed unless it is absolutely necessary."

The meeting stretched late into the night, the details of their plan falling into place like pieces of a puzzle. But as Elara dismissed her advisors and stood to leave the chamber, a sudden thought struck her. Was she too late? Was the rot already so deep that even her best efforts would be in vain?

The enemy within was not a force that could be defeated with swords and shields. It was a sickness, a betrayal that ate away at the very foundation of her rule. She had always known that the path to power was fraught with peril, but she had never imagined that the true threat would come from those she had trusted the most.

As she stood at the window, gazing out over the kingdom that was slowly slipping from her grasp, Elara made a silent vow. She would not let her bloodline be the undoing of everything she had worked for. The enemy within had shown itself, and now she would fight back with everything she had. There would be no mercy for those who sought to destroy her.

○ The Unlikely Allies

In the cold, darkened halls of Castle Valiara, where the stone walls seemed to whisper of past betrayals, Elara stood before the ancient map, her fingers tracing the intricate lines that divided the lands. The kingdom, once united under the bloodline of the Bloodborn, now lay fractured, torn apart by forces she could barely comprehend. She had fought against enemies from within and beyond, yet nothing had prepared her for the alliances she would have to forge to survive the coming storm.

The gathering was set. The allies she had summoned were not those she would have chosen in any other circumstance. They were the last of the Bloodborn's enemies—former adversaries who had once sought her downfall. Now, in the face of a greater threat, they were her only hope.

First to arrive was Kieran, the Black Sword of Falgrim. His reputation as a ruthless mercenary was well-earned, and his sword had stained more blood than Elara cared to count. He was tall, with a grim expression that never seemed to leave his face. His cold eyes never met hers, only scanning the room, as if searching for any hint of weakness. The room was thick with tension as Kieran stood in the corner, his dark cloak trailing behind him like a shadow.

Next, Leandra arrived, her long silver hair cascading like a waterfall of moonlight, her green eyes sharp and calculating. The former Lady of Mirathis, she had once conspired against the throne itself, aligning herself with forces that sought to destroy the very heart of Elara's kingdom. Now, that same kingdom stood on the brink of collapse, and her knowledge of court intrigues and magic was now an invaluable asset. Her entrance was silent, yet her presence was unmistakable. She was a woman who commanded attention, and no one dared to underestimate her.

Lastly, the most surprising arrival was Darian, a former priest of the Celestial Order, whose faith had once been the foundation of his strength. A year ago, he had denounced everything he had sworn to protect, abandoning his vows in search of forbidden power. He now stood before Elara as a man broken by his own ambition, his once-pure eyes clouded by the weight of the dark magic he had embraced. His presence felt heavy, the air growing colder as he stepped into the room.

Elara stared at the three figures before her, all once enemies, now her only hope. She had spent countless sleepless nights wondering how this moment would unfold, and now it was here. The shadows of the past loomed large, but the future was even darker. If they were to survive, they would need to trust each other—something none of them had ever done before.

"We stand at the precipice of destruction," Elara began, her voice steady but carrying the weight of a thousand lives. "The forces we face are not of this world. They are older, more powerful, and they will stop at nothing to see us destroyed. If we do not work together, we will fall, each of us alone, like so many before us."

Kieran's eyes glinted with skepticism. "I don't trust any of you," he said, his voice low and filled with a cold edge. "But I'm not in this for trust. I'm in this for survival."

Leandra's lips curled into a smile, though it was anything but warm. "Trust is a luxury we cannot afford," she said. "What matters now is power, and how we wield it."

Darian, ever the enigma, stared at the ground for a long moment before lifting his gaze to meet Elara's. "There is no honor in what we are about to do," he murmured, his voice heavy with regret. "But honor will not save us."

The silence that followed was palpable, thick with the weight of their shared history and the uncertain future that awaited them. Elara knew that this was only the beginning. They had no choice but to fight together, to stand side by side against an enemy that knew no mercy.

With a deep breath, Elara finally spoke, her voice cutting through the tension like a blade. "Then let us make this alliance. Not for honor, not for glory, but for the survival of our people. We are the last hope of this kingdom."

Each of them nodded, understanding the gravity of the moment. They were enemies turned allies, bound by the same cause, yet still prisoners of their pasts. As the map of the kingdom lay before them, Elara knew that the true battle was not just against the enemy at their gates—but against the darkness within themselves. Only time would tell if they could overcome their pasts and emerge victorious.

For now, however, the only thing that mattered was that they had come together. And together, they would face whatever horrors awaited them in the shadows.

The tension in the room lingered as the four of them gathered around the map, a heavy silence settling between them. Elara's mind raced, her thoughts weaving through the endless possibilities and strategies, but she knew that this fragile alliance would be tested far beyond any battle they had ever fought. Each of them had scars that ran deep—scars that were not easily forgotten or forgiven.

Kieran's hand rested on the hilt of his sword, his fingers twitching slightly as though he could not resist the urge to unsheathe it at any moment. He had always fought for the highest bidder, for the thrill of the kill, not for honor or righteousness. He was a weapon, and nothing more. But in this moment, something in his cold demeanor seemed to shift ever so slightly.

Leandra's gaze was fixed on the map, her fingers tracing the lines of the kingdom's borders, though her thoughts seemed far away. She had once been a queen, an orchestrator of plots and schemes that had crumbled kingdoms. The blood of her enemies stained her hands, and there was no telling what she would sacrifice now. She had always been a player in the game of power, but with the shadows closing in, the stakes had changed. Now, survival was the only currency she had left.

Darian stood apart from the rest, as always, his thoughts a labyrinth that none could navigate. Once a man of faith, his eyes no longer held the light of belief but the darkness of something far more dangerous. The magic he wielded now was not of the divine, but of the forbidden, drawn from forces that could consume him entirely if he wasn't careful. His past was his own prison, but he was also their key to defeating what lay ahead.

"Tell me again what we're up against," Kieran finally spoke, his voice breaking the silence that had stretched too long. His eyes flickered toward Elara, challenging her to offer some semblance of clarity.

Elara didn't flinch. She had known this moment would come—the moment when the menacing unknowns would need to be laid bare. She had to trust them, even if they hadn't earned it. They had no other choice.

"The enemy is not of our world," she began, her voice steady but heavy with the gravity of the truth she now had to face. "It's something older. Something that predates the Bloodborn. The Varnath, as they call themselves, have returned. They are an ancient race, long thought extinct, but they are not. They've been waiting, gathering power, and now, they are ready to strike."

Darian's eyes narrowed, his lips curling into a faint, bitter smile. "The Varnath... their magic is forbidden. It was sealed away for a reason."

Leandra's expression darkened as she studied the map again. "Sealed away, yes. But they have found a way to break the seal. This is no longer about kingdoms or thrones. This is about the very fabric of our world. If the Varnath succeed, everything will fall."

Kieran's grip on his sword tightened, his voice low and dangerous. "And you trust us? After all we've done to each other? You think we can just put aside our history and fight together?"

Elara met his gaze, her own eyes hardening. "We have no choice. We are not here for the past. We are here because the future demands it."

Darian stepped forward, his voice carrying a quiet intensity. "There are things the Varnath can do that none of us could ever dream of. They can turn the living into shadows, manipulate the minds of men, and twist time itself. Their power knows no bounds."

Leandra's lips parted in a silent exhale, her fingers trembling slightly as they hovered over the map. "Then we must strike first. We cannot wait for them to come to us."

Kieran nodded slowly, a glimmer of agreement in his eyes. "I've never been one to wait. Let's show them how this world fights."

Elara surveyed the room, her heart pounding in her chest. She had no illusions about what lay ahead. They were not just fighting an enemy; they were fighting the very nature of their world. The Varnath sought to unravel the threads that held the kingdoms together, to turn everything into chaos. To win, they would have to work together, despite their differences.

"This will not be easy," Elara said, her voice breaking the silence once more. "We will face trials that will test us all. We will lose people. But we will not lose this war. Not while we have the strength to fight."

The room fell into a heavy silence again, as each of them processed what had just been said. They knew what they had to do. There was no turning back now. The choice had been made, and though their bond was forged in desperation and mutual need, there was no other path but forward.

"Then let's begin," Kieran said, his voice gruff but resolute.

And so, their unlikely alliance was sealed, not in friendship or honor, but in the grim determination to survive. Together, they would face the darkness—together, they would stand against the Varnath, no matter the cost.

Part III: The Final Reckoning

1. The War of Shadows

- The Battle Begins

The first rumblings of war were like distant thunder, growing louder with each passing hour, as if the very earth itself trembled in anticipation of the violence to come. Elara stood at the balcony of the palace, her gaze fixed on the horizon, where the sky was streaked with the red and gold hues of the setting sun. It should have been a peaceful evening, a time for reflection, but the weight of what lay ahead hung heavily on her shoulders.

Her kingdom, once a place of prosperity and peace, was now on the brink of destruction. The betrayal within her court, the rising power of Vanguard, and the ancient curse that still clung to her bloodline had set the stage for a conflict unlike any the realm had ever known. A final battle was inevitable. It was not a matter of if, but when.

The sound of footsteps behind her broke her reverie. She didn't need to turn to know who it was. Calen, her most trusted general, stood at her side, his presence a quiet but unshakable strength. He had been with her since the beginning, through the darkest moments of her reign. She could feel the tension in the air around him, just as she felt it within herself.

"Your Majesty," he began, his voice low but steady, "the forces are ready. The first wave of Vanguard's troops is approaching. We've stationed our defenses along the western front, but I fear their numbers are too great."

Elara closed her eyes for a moment, steadying herself. "Then we fight," she said, her voice firm. "We fight, not just for our kingdom, but for everything we have left to protect." She turned to face him, her expression a mixture of resolve and sorrow. "Gather the men. We move at dawn."

The war had already begun, but it was not just a war of armies. It was a war of ideologies, of bloodlines, and of fate. Vanguard, led by the enigmatic Lord Malgor, had long harbored ambitions to overthrow Elara's rule, and with each passing day, those ambitions had turned into a twisted obsession. The lands of the kingdom, once united under the banner of the Queen, were now divided, the once loyal subjects torn between allegiance to their ruler and the promises of power offered by the rebels.

In the Great Hall, Elara's council convened in tense silence. Each member of her inner circle bore the weight of the coming conflict. Rhiannon, the royal sorceress, stood near the hearth, her dark eyes glowing with a strange intensity. She had warned them of the dangers that lay ahead, of the dark magic that flowed through the veins of the Bloodborn, but even she could not foresee the true extent of the battle that was unfolding.

"It's more than just a war of soldiers," Rhiannon said, her voice carrying the heaviness of a prophecy. "It is the culmination of everything we have feared. The curse upon your bloodline has awakened, Elara. And with it, something far worse than we have ever known."

Elara's grip tightened on the armrest of her chair. "I know. I feel it. The darkness is stirring, and it is stronger than before. But we must stand, Rhiannon. We cannot let fear control us."

As the night wore on, the flickering of the torches cast long shadows on the stone walls, the flickers of flame reflecting the uncertainty and anxiety that gripped the hearts of those present. The room was filled with the murmurs of the council, each advisor and ally weighing the choices ahead. But amidst the uncertainty, one thing was clear: Elara could no longer hesitate. The battle was no longer a distant threat—it was here, and there was no turning back.

Dawn came, breaking the darkness with a fierce, golden light that cast the battlefield in stark relief. The land stretched out before Elara like a vast, unforgiving expanse, where the lives of countless souls would soon be decided. She stood at the head of her forces, her heart racing with a mixture of fear and determination. This was not just her kingdom at stake; this was the survival of everything she had ever known.

"Remember why we fight," she called to her soldiers, her voice carrying over the wind. "We fight for our homes, our families, and our future. We fight because there is no other choice."

The army of Vanguard appeared on the horizon, a dark mass that seemed to blot out the sun itself. Malgor's forces were vast, but Elara's army was loyal—each soldier willing to lay down their life for their queen. As the first clash of swords rang out, the ground beneath them seemed to shake with the force of their fury. It was only the beginning.

The battle was chaos. The clash of steel, the cries of the fallen, and the screams of those still fighting filled the air. Elara fought alongside her generals, her blade cutting through the thick of the enemy lines. Her heart was heavy with the weight of leadership, but her spirit was unbroken. She had no choice but to lead them forward. The stakes had never been higher.

Calen fought by her side, his eyes fierce with determination. "The left flank is collapsing!" he shouted over the din of battle. "We need to reinforce them!"

Without hesitation, Elara gave the command. The battle raged on, each moment more desperate than the last. But in the midst of the bloodshed, Elara saw a glimmer of something in the distance—something far more dangerous than any soldier or weapon.

A shadow moved in the trees, a figure cloaked in dark robes. Rhiannon's warning echoed in her mind. The dark magic was here.

As the battle pressed on, Elara realized that this was not just a fight for her kingdom—it was a fight for her very soul. Every swing of her sword, every command she gave, carried the weight of an ancient curse, one that threatened to consume everything she loved.

But she was no longer the uncertain queen who had ascended to the throne. She was Elara, the Bloodborn Queen. And she would fight until her last breath, for her kingdom, her people, and for the hope that remained in the heart of every soldier on the battlefield.

The battle would not be won in a single day. But it would be remembered for generations. And as the sun set over the blood-soaked earth, Elara knew that this was only the beginning. The real reckoning was yet to come.

The battle had raged through the day, and as the sun began to dip beneath the horizon, the world seemed to grow colder, darker, more ominous. The clash of steel had subsided, replaced by the steady, haunting cries of the wounded and dying. The battlefield was a grim mosaic of broken armor, shattered shields, and bodies strewn across the earth like fallen leaves. The once-pristine land was now tainted with the blood of both the innocent and the guilty, an inescapable testament to the brutality of war.

Elara stood at the edge of the battlefield, her armor slick with the blood of her enemies, her breath coming in short, ragged gasps. Her sword, now heavy in her hand, was coated in the dark stains of battle. The sun's fading light cast long shadows across the ground, distorting the fallen figures into grotesque shapes. She had been a queen, a ruler who had prided herself on diplomacy, on maintaining the fragile peace of her kingdom. But now, in this moment, she was a warrior, and her heart had hardened to the relentless reality of war.

She had fought valiantly, leading her soldiers with the strength and courage that only a true monarch could muster. Yet, even as her forces held their ground, the overwhelming force of Vanguard had taken its toll. The western flank, the one that had collapsed earlier, had been reinforced, but it had come at a cost. Countless lives had been lost, and with each fallen soldier, Elara's resolve began to feel the strain.

Calen appeared at her side, his expression grim as he surveyed the battlefield. "Your Majesty, we've pushed them back for now, but they'll regroup. We need to pull back and consolidate our forces. We can't afford another assault like this."

Elara's gaze remained fixed on the horizon, her mind racing. "We can't afford to retreat. If we pull back now, it will be a sign of weakness. Vanguard will have the upper hand, and they will never stop coming."

"You're right," Calen replied, his voice low and filled with concern. "But if we don't rest, if we don't tend to our wounded and regroup, we'll be in no shape to fight another day. We must think of the long-term strategy, not just the battle in front of us."

For a long moment, Elara was silent, torn between her instinct to press forward and the harsh reality of the situation. The soldiers under her command were exhausted, their spirits battered by the endless onslaught. Yet, she could feel the pulse of something deeper, a fire that refused to be extinguished. She had led them this far, and she could not let them falter now.

"We make our stand here," Elara said, her voice unwavering. "We will rest for a short while, but we don't retreat. Vanguard must know that we are unyielding. The fight is far from over."

As night fell, the camp was filled with the sounds of soldiers tending to the wounded, their faces drawn and weary, their eyes haunted by the horrors they had witnessed. Fires flickered in the distance, their glow casting an eerie light across the land. Elara stood at the edge of the camp, watching as the last remnants of daylight disappeared. The world was quiet, save for the murmurs of her soldiers and the crackling of the flames.

But it wasn't peace that she found in the silence. It was a growing sense of dread. The dark magic that had been creeping through the air like a slow poison was becoming palpable. She could feel it, a presence in the air that made her skin crawl, something ancient and malevolent that lurked just beyond the veil of the world she knew. It was a force that none of her people understood, but one that she had been warned about time and time again.

Rhiannon appeared at her side, her face pale, her eyes wide with unspoken fear. The sorceress had always been the voice of reason, the one who could sense things that others could not, but tonight, there was something in her gaze that unsettled Elara.

"Elara," Rhiannon whispered, her voice barely audible above the noise of the camp. "It's not just Vanguard we're fighting. There is something else—something far darker than we could have ever imagined."

"What do you mean?" Elara asked, turning to face her with a frown. She had heard the warnings, but this was the first time Rhiannon had spoken of it so openly.

"I've felt it for days," Rhiannon said, her voice trembling. "The magic in the air is growing stronger. The curse... it is awakening. And it is tied to something far older than even the Bloodborn curse. Something that has been buried for centuries, waiting for the right moment to rise again."

Elara's heart sank. She had known that the ancient bloodline she carried held a terrible secret, but to hear Rhiannon speak of it in such dire terms only deepened her fear. What had she unwittingly unleashed by standing in the way of Vanguard's rise?

"Elara, you must understand," Rhiannon continued, her voice trembling with urgency. "This is not just about reclaiming your throne. This is about saving your soul—and the souls of all who follow you."

The weight of her words hung in the air like a storm cloud, dark and oppressive. Elara's mind raced, but she knew one thing for certain:

the war was no longer just a fight for power. It was a battle for survival, not just of her kingdom, but of the very essence of who she was.

The next day, as the first light of dawn touched the battlefield once more, Elara gathered her forces for what would surely be the final clash. The landscape was eerily silent, as though the earth itself held its breath in anticipation of what was to come. Vanguard's army, though bloodied and battered from the previous day's clash, was still formidable, still driven by the ambition of their leader, Lord Malgor.

But Elara could feel the weight of fate pressing down on her. This was not just a battle of armies; this was the culmination of all the ancient powers that had shaped her kingdom, and it was a battle that would define her legacy.

The last clash would determine whether the shadows of her past would be extinguished—or whether they would rise once again to consume everything she had fought for.

And so, with a battle cry that echoed across the land, Elara and her army prepared to face the greatest trial of their lives. The battle was far from over.

- The Queen's Command

Elara stood on the balcony of her royal chambers, her eyes scanning the horizon where the last traces of daylight faded into the deepening dusk. The once vibrant skies were now heavy with a sense of foreboding, a reflection of the turmoil that gripped the kingdom. The world seemed to be holding its breath, waiting for something—something inevitable—to unfold. Her heart, however, was already racing. She could feel it in the pit of her stomach, the tension in the air that only those born of blood could understand.

The throne had never felt heavier than it did in that moment. As a child, she had dreamed of this power, but she had never imagined the weight of it would feel so suffocating. And yet, as much as she resented the responsibilities that came with it, Elara knew there was no turning back. She was the Queen now. She had inherited a crown soaked in the blood of her ancestors, and with it came a duty that neither time nor circumstance could erase. The kingdom, fragile as it was, depended on her decisions. The people, once loyal and thriving under her father's rule, now looked to her for salvation.

Her thoughts were interrupted by the heavy, deliberate sound of boots on stone. She turned, her gaze locking onto the figure that stepped into her chambers—Seraphus, her most trusted advisor. His tall frame was imposing, his dark eyes sharp, betraying none of the emotion he might have been feeling. His presence was always a reminder of the war they had been fighting long before the armies had even gathered on the borders.

"Your Majesty," Seraphus began, bowing slightly. His voice was steady, but there was a flicker of something unreadable beneath the surface. "The council has assembled. They await your word."

Elara nodded, brushing a strand of her raven-black hair behind her ear. It had been a long day, filled with reports of dissent, whispers of rebellion, and murmurs of a rebellion from within her own ranks. The royal court had long been a place of intrigue and ambition, but now, it was a powder keg. And she was the one holding the match.

"Very well," she replied, her voice calm but firm. "Prepare the hall. I will address them now."

Seraphus hesitated, stepping forward slightly. "Your Majesty, if I may," he said, his voice low, "there are matters of great urgency you must consider. The Vanguard's movements grow bolder by the day. They have made no attempt to conceal their plans."

Elara's gaze hardened, her hands clenching at her sides. The Vanguard, a name that had haunted her dreams ever since she was a child, was not just a group of rebels—they were a force that could tear the kingdom apart if not dealt with swiftly. Her bloodline was marked by their cursed actions, and now, their shadows loomed larger than ever before.

"I am aware of the Vanguard," she said, her tone icy. "And I know the cost of their defiance. But we cannot let fear control us. I will not cower in the face of those who believe they can take what is mine."

The finality in her words left no room for debate. Seraphus did not argue, but his expression betrayed a flicker of doubt. He had always been a cautious man, calculating in his every move. But Elara had changed. The woman who had once doubted her own strength was gone, replaced by someone who would stop at nothing to ensure her kingdom's survival.

She straightened her back, her eyes now burning with resolve.

"Gather the generals," she commanded. "Prepare for war."

Seraphus nodded, bowing once more before leaving the room. As the door closed behind him, Elara took a deep breath, allowing the weight of the decision to settle on her shoulders. There was no turning back now. The blood of her ancestors had called her to this moment, and she would answer with everything she had.

The kingdom would be hers to protect. And anyone who threatened that would face her wrath.

Elara moved to the ornate mirror across the room, her reflection staring back at her with a mixture of determination and an edge of something else—something she had kept hidden even from herself. The face of a queen, yes, but beneath the crown, beneath the regal attire, was a woman who had been forged in the fires of loss, of betrayal, and of the constant pressure to be perfect. She had lost much in her life, but one thing she knew with absolute certainty was that she would not lose her kingdom.

A knock at the door interrupted her thoughts. Without waiting for permission, the heavy oak door swung open, revealing Seraphus standing with a grim expression.

"Your Majesty," he said, stepping inside, "the generals are ready, and the council awaits your arrival. But..." He hesitated, the weight of the unspoken words heavy in the air.

"But what?" Elara's voice was sharp, her patience thinning as the hours passed. She was already stretched thin, the weight of the upcoming decisions pressing down on her.

"The council... they are split," Seraphus continued. "Some believe we should make an alliance with the Vanguard, or at least negotiate. They are under the impression that the bloodshed can be avoided. But I fear their hope is misplaced."

Elara's eyes narrowed as she turned away from the mirror, her face a mask of cold resolve. "The Vanguard have shown no interest in peace. They want chaos. They want to destroy everything we stand for, and if we allow them to breathe even for a moment, they will destroy us. Negotiation is a weakness, and I will not let my kingdom fall to cowardice."

Seraphus nodded silently, his expression resigned. He knew Elara well enough to understand that once her mind was made up, there was no changing it. Yet, the unease still lingered in his eyes.

"Shall we proceed, then?" he asked.

Elara took a long, steadying breath. The queen she had become—unforgiving, relentless—was not the woman she had once been, but it was the woman she had to be now. She had learned long ago that compassion could only go so far when the very survival of her people was on the line.

"Yes," she said firmly. "Lead me to the council. We have no time to waste."

As they walked through the grand hallways of the royal palace, each step felt heavier than the last. The murmurs of servants and soldiers echoed faintly in the distance, but here, in the heart of the palace, it was always silent. Only the footsteps of the queen and her closest advisors filled the void.

The council chamber was a place of solemn importance, its tall, arched windows overlooking the sprawling city below. The room was lined with tapestries that told the stories of battles won and lost, a reminder of the legacy she now carried. The air inside was thick with tension, the nobles and generals seated at a long, polished table, their faces a mixture of hope and fear.

When Elara entered, all conversation ceased. Every pair of eyes turned toward her—some with respect, some with skepticism. She had known from the beginning that not everyone in the court had accepted her as their true queen. But this was her moment to prove them wrong.

She took her seat at the head of the table, her posture regal and unyielding. Seraphus stood beside her, his presence a silent reassurance that her decisions would be backed by strength.

"Let us make one thing clear," Elara began, her voice calm but unwavering, "The Vanguard will not be given the chance to cripple this kingdom. I will not bow to them, and I will not bend in the face of their threats. If they want war, they shall have it."

A murmur spread through the room, and one of the older council members, Lord Ferran, spoke up. His tone was cautious but pointed.

"But Your Majesty, the Vanguard is not the only enemy we face. The kingdom is divided. There are factions within our own walls that do not see eye to eye with your rule. If we go to war with the Vanguard, we risk losing more than just men on the battlefield. We risk losing the very heart of this kingdom."

Elara met his gaze, her expression hardening. "And if we do not act, Lord Ferran, we risk losing everything. There is no middle ground. The Vanguard is a threat that cannot be ignored. If you are unwilling to take the necessary steps to protect our people, then I suggest you leave the room before I make my final decision."

The room fell silent, the weight of her words hanging in the air. No one dared to speak again, and Elara could see the subtle shifts in the faces of the council members. Some had turned pale, while others seemed to grow even more resolute in their stance. There were those who feared her, but more importantly, there were those who feared the consequences of not following her command.

The queen had made her position clear. The only question now was whether the council would follow her lead, or whether they would face the consequences of their inaction.

As the silence stretched on, Elara's mind was already racing ahead. The Vanguard was only one of many challenges. Her father's enemies still lurked in the shadows, and even within her own walls, treachery and discontent festered. But she was no longer the uncertain heir who once cowered under the weight of her father's legacy. She was the queen. And she would shape this kingdom by her will, no matter the cost.

"Prepare the armies," Elara finally said, breaking the silence. "We march at dawn."

The council was left in stunned silence as Elara rose from her seat, the echoes of her command reverberating through the stone walls. There was no turning back now. The queen had spoken. And the fate of the kingdom rested in her hands.

○ The Tide Turns

The tide of battle shifted in an instant, as though the very winds of fate had turned against them. Elara stood on the battlefield, her heart heavy with the weight of the choices she had made, yet resolute. The din of clashing swords, the cries of dying soldiers, and the crackle of magic in the air surrounded her, but in that moment, all she could hear was the pounding of her own pulse in her ears.

The Vanguard had been relentless in their assault, a storm of fury sweeping across the kingdom. Elara had called upon every ounce of strength within her, each spell, each command, each strategy, designed to hold back the tide of darkness. But it had not been enough. The enemy had learned from past mistakes. They had adapted, and now they stood on the edge of victory.

But Elara refused to yield. She had seen the faces of her people—the fear, the despair—and it spurred her on. They believed in her. They had followed her through every trial, and now it was her turn to give everything she had. Her eyes locked onto the figure of Rhiannon, her most trusted advisor, standing beside her, just as determined.

"We cannot let them break through," Elara said, her voice cold and steady despite the chaos. Rhiannon nodded, her expression grim but unshaken. They both knew that this was more than just a battle—it was the future of their kingdom at stake.

"Ready the Crimson Guard," Rhiannon called to the nearest captain, who quickly relayed the orders. The elite warriors, who had stood by Elara's side since the beginning of her reign, began to move into position, forming a line of defense that would give their queen the time she needed.

Elara's fingers danced through the air, weaving the ancient magic of her bloodline, calling upon the power that had sustained her ancestors for centuries. The ground beneath her feet trembled, the air thick with the tension of impending destruction. With a sharp, fluid motion, she raised her hands to the sky, and a blinding light erupted from the earth, sweeping across the battlefield like a tidal wave.

For a moment, the enemy faltered. The Vanguard, their ranks shaken by the unexpected assault, hesitated, their momentum faltering. The soldiers of Elara's army seized the opportunity, charging forward with renewed strength, their resolve hardened by the sudden reversal.

It was then that Elara saw it—the moment they had all been waiting for. In the distance, the banner of the Crimson Guard flew high, the last bastion of hope in this war. It was a symbol of their defiance, their unwillingness to submit to the shadows that sought to consume them.

With a roar, Elara charged alongside her soldiers, her sword raised high, the blade gleaming in the fading light. Her heart burned with the fire of a queen who had nothing left to lose, and everything to gain.

The enemy had underestimated her, underestimated the power of her people.

But the tide had indeed turned. And it would never return to the way it had been.

As she cut her way through the ranks of the Vanguard, Elara's mind raced with thoughts of the cost of victory. The battle was far from over, but the spark of hope had been rekindled. And as long as there was hope, there was still a chance to turn the darkness back.

In that moment, she knew one thing for certain: This was her kingdom, and she would fight for it with every breath in her body.

The clash of steel against steel rang in her ears as Elara pressed forward, her every step fueled by the urgency of the battle. The Vanguard, though momentarily thrown off balance by her magic, were quick to regroup, their ruthless discipline reasserting itself. Elara's soldiers fought with fervor, their spirits lifted by the sudden shift, but she knew the war was far from won. This was but a single moment in a far larger struggle.

Her eyes scanned the battlefield, searching for the commanders of the enemy. She needed to strike at the heart of their leadership to truly cripple their forces. Her gaze locked on a figure atop a nearby hill—an armored man with a black banner swirling in the wind. That was Kaldar, the leader of the Vanguard, the one who had orchestrated the bloodshed. If they could take him down, the rest would crumble.

"Elara, wait!" Rhiannon shouted, her voice cutting through the noise of battle.

Elara turned, meeting her advisor's gaze with a fierce determination. "I have to finish this. He's the key."

Rhiannon's face tightened with worry. "You know the risks. You're already stretched too thin. We need you alive to lead us through the aftermath."

Elara clenched her fists, feeling the weight of Rhiannon's words. Her magic was already starting to wane, the immense toll of drawing upon her bloodline's power beginning to take its toll. But the fire within her would not be extinguished so easily. She had come too far to falter now.

"I'm not letting them take everything," Elara said, her voice low but filled with unwavering resolve. "This ends today."

Rhiannon hesitated, then nodded, understanding the depth of her queen's determination. "Then we follow you, as always."

With that, they charged together, side by side, cutting a path through the enemy forces as they made their way toward Kaldar. The Vanguard soldiers, skilled and battle-hardened, tried to intercept them, but Elara's fury was a force in itself. Each swing of her blade carried the weight of her kingdom's survival, each strike a promise that the shadows would not claim her people.

The battlefield stretched out before her like a dark sea, and Elara pushed forward, her heart racing as she neared the top of the hill where Kaldar waited. He was a towering figure, his armor as dark as the night itself, his sword gleaming with an unnatural aura. He had been the architect of the bloodshed, the one who had twisted the ancient magics to suit his purpose. Now, the time for reckoning had come.

Kaldar saw her approach, and his lips curled into a cruel smile. "So, the queen comes to face me herself," he mocked. "You think your magic can save you? You are nothing more than a puppet, Elara. A puppet of the past."

Elara stopped just a few paces from him, her breath shallow but her stance unwavering. "You may control the darkness, Kaldar," she said, her voice steady, "but you cannot break what is not yours."

With a roar, Kaldar lunged, his blade cutting through the air with deadly precision. Elara met his strike with a clash of steel, sparks flying as their swords collided. The force of the impact reverberated through her arm, but she did not falter. She had fought too long, too hard, to be intimidated now.

Each strike she delivered was calculated, each movement driven by the need to protect her people, to keep the kingdom alive. But Kaldar was no novice. His dark powers surged through him, enhancing his strength and speed, turning him into a beast of battle. Elara could feel the pressure mounting, her strength slowly ebbing as her magic drained from the exertion.

"You cannot win this, Elara," Kaldar hissed, pressing forward with renewed fury. "The bloodline's power will be mine, and with it, I will tear this world apart."

Elara's gaze hardened. She could feel the weight of her ancestors' power, deep within her, and she knew that the final victory lay not in the strength of her magic, but in the conviction of her will.

With a fierce cry, Elara summoned every ounce of power left within her, focusing the ancient magic into a single, overwhelming blast. The force of it shattered the air, sending a shockwave rippling through the battlefield. Kaldar's blade faltered, and in that instant, Elara drove her sword through his chest, piercing his heart with the same unwavering resolve that had carried her through every trial.

The battlefield fell into an eerie silence as Kaldar crumpled to the ground, his life extinguished by the very magic he had sought to control. Elara stood over him, her chest heaving with exhaustion, her sword dripping with the blood of her enemy. The darkness that had loomed over the kingdom was beginning to dissipate, the tide finally turning in their favor.

But even as the enemy forces faltered, Elara knew that this victory, though hard-won, was only the beginning. The war was not over, and the cost of it would be felt for generations to come. Yet, as she looked out across the battlefield, she felt a surge of hope, the first spark of light breaking through the storm.

The queen had survived. And the tide had turned.

2. The Price of Power

- The Heart of Betrayal

The chill of the night settled heavily over the kingdom, a stark contrast to the warmth of the once-thriving court. Elara stood in the center of her chamber, her hands trembling as she stared at the letter before her. The wax seal, broken and revealing the grim message inside, carried the weight of something she hadn't fully expected. Betrayal. It was never a word she thought would taint her reign, but there it was, staring her in the face.

The ink on the parchment seemed to bleed with the gravity of the words: "The throne is in danger. They move against you, Elara. And it is someone you trust."

Her breath caught in her throat. *Trust.* That had always been the foundation of her rule, the silent pact between her and those closest to her. She had given it freely, expecting loyalty in return. But now, in this cold hour, that very loyalty had turned hollow.

Across the room, the dark figure of Orin, her most trusted advisor, stood in silence. His presence was always a comfort, yet tonight, it felt like an imposition. His hands were folded behind his back, his posture rigid, as if he knew what she was about to face but refused to speak of it.

Elara's voice, barely above a whisper, broke the silence. "Orin, do you know of this?"

His face was unreadable, but the faintest twitch in his jaw betrayed him. He had known. She didn't need to ask again. She could see it in his eyes.

"You don't have to do this," she continued, her voice stronger now, though the weight of doubt was growing inside her. "You were my friend. My ally. How could you—"

"Elara," Orin interrupted softly, stepping closer. His tone was calm, but there was an edge to it. "The path you walk, the one you chose when you took the throne, has never been a straight one. The bloodline you carry... it demands more than you can give. And I, too, am bound by forces you do not understand."

The words hit her like a physical blow. She had always known there was more to Orin than he let on, but to hear him admit it, to feel the truth of it seeping into the very air they shared, left her feeling hollow.

"How long?" she asked, her eyes narrowing as she searched his face for any sign of remorse.

"Long enough to see where the kingdom was headed," he replied. "Long enough to understand that your rule, for all its promise, will only lead to bloodshed. A change must come."

Elara stepped back, her heart racing. *A change?* Was that what this was about? Orin, the one person she believed could never falter, was now her greatest adversary. The betrayal wasn't just in his actions; it was in the realization that the very person who had sworn to protect her was now aligned with the forces that sought to destroy everything she had built.

"I will not let you destroy what I've worked for," Elara said firmly, her voice a low growl. "I will fight this, Orin. I will fight you."

He looked at her with a mix of pity and regret. "You don't understand, Elara. This war—this betrayal—it was never about you. It was about the blood that runs through your veins. The power it holds."

The room felt colder now, and Elara's mind raced. She had always believed in the power of the crown, the strength of her lineage. But now, faced with Orin's betrayal, the very foundation of her rule seemed fragile, as though it could shatter with the slightest misstep.

"You were never my ally," she whispered, the sting of realization cutting deeper than any blade. "You were always playing me."

Orin's face softened slightly, his eyes clouded with the sorrow of a man forced to choose between loyalty and ambition. "I never wanted it to come to this, Elara. But sometimes, there is no choice."

As Elara stood there, the weight of his words pressing down on her chest, she knew that this was only the beginning. The heart of betrayal had been revealed, and it beat within the walls of her most trusted circle. There was no turning back now. The kingdom was on the brink, and she would either rise above this treachery or be consumed by it.

Her heart hardened. The war was no longer just against her enemies; it was now a war for her very survival. And she would not allow anyone, not even Orin, to take that from her.

"Then let it begin," she said, her voice steely and unwavering. "Let the reckoning come."

The days that followed were marked by an oppressive silence in the castle, as if the very walls were holding their breath, waiting for the inevitable clash. Elara had retreated into her private chambers, her mind a whirlwind of conflicting emotions. Every move she made, every decision she pondered, was now overshadowed by the bitter sting of Orin's betrayal. Yet, amidst the chaos of her thoughts, one truth stood clear: the battle for her throne had already begun, and she had no choice but to play the game, no matter the cost.

She summoned her most trusted generals, those few who remained loyal, to the war room late that evening. The flickering torchlight cast long shadows on the stone walls, as though the very atmosphere in the room was thick with treachery. But Elara was resolute. She had to act swiftly, before her enemies, now emboldened by Orin's defection, could rally their forces against her.

General Kael, a tall, stern man with a sharp mind and a quiet strength, stood at her side, his hands clasped behind his back as he studied the map laid out before them. His face was impassive, but Elara could see the tension in his posture, the same tension she felt in her bones.

"Elara," Kael began, his voice low but steady, "we need to prepare for the worst. If Orin has aligned himself with our enemies, the threat to the throne is more immediate than we realized. His influence extends far beyond this castle."

Elara nodded, her mind already racing through the various options available to her. She had always prided herself on her strategic thinking, but now, with betrayal festering in her closest circle, every choice seemed fraught with danger.

"Tell me what you know of the forces at play," she ordered, her voice calm, but with an underlying steel.

Kael unfolded the map further, pointing to the northern border where the kingdom's most vulnerable flank lay. "The rebels, led by Lord Farrick, have already begun to gather troops. If Orin has thrown his support behind them, they will have the resources they need to strike swiftly. We cannot afford to wait."

Elara's fingers traced the map as Kael spoke, her thoughts racing. She knew Farrick's name all too well. A nobleman once loyal to the crown, he had grown disillusioned with her rule and had defected years ago, leading a small but growing faction of disgruntled nobles and soldiers. It had been a thorn in her side for years, but now, with Orin's betrayal, Farrick would be more dangerous than ever.

"We need to move first," Elara said, her voice firm. "We strike before they can mobilize. Gather the troops. We'll hit Farrick's stronghold at dawn."

Kael hesitated, his brow furrowing. "A direct assault could be risky, Elara. Farrick knows how to defend his territory. It would be wiser to wait for reinforcements."

"No," Elara interrupted sharply, her eyes flashing with a fire that matched the determination in her voice. "Waiting is not an option. We cannot afford to give them time to strengthen their position. If we hesitate now, we may lose everything. I will not let Orin's betrayal define my reign."

Kael studied her for a long moment, as if weighing the cost of her decision. Finally, he nodded. "As you command."

The following day, Elara rode out with her army, her resolve as unyielding as the sword at her side. The air was crisp, the sky a dull gray, as if the heavens themselves were watching with a somber gaze. The soldiers marched in tight formation, their faces grim, but there was no question about their loyalty. They followed her because they believed in her, and she would not fail them.

As they neared Lord Farrick's stronghold, Elara could feel the weight of the moment pressing down on her. This was more than just a military engagement—it was a test of her strength, her resolve, and her ability to overcome the deepest betrayal. Every step forward was a step further into a world of uncertainty and danger. But she could not afford to falter. Not now.

The battle unfolded quickly, as Kael had predicted. Farrick's forces had fortified their position, but they were not prepared for the speed and precision of Elara's assault. Her troops, trained for such rapid engagements, breached the outer walls with ease, and within hours, the stronghold was under siege.

Yet, as Elara stood in the midst of the chaos, her sword slick with the blood of her enemies, she couldn't shake the feeling that this victory was hollow. Every victory she claimed from now on would be tainted by the betrayal of Orin, the man she had trusted above all others.

In the heat of the battle, Elara's thoughts drifted back to Orin. He had been her closest confidant, the one who had stood by her side through every challenge, every triumph. But now, his name was a curse on her lips. *How could he do this?* She could not understand it, no matter how hard she tried.

As the last of Farrick's forces were driven back, Elara stood over the battlefield, her chest heaving with exertion. The victory was hers, but the war had only just begun. The betrayal that had begun in the heart of her court had now spread to the very fabric of her kingdom. And she would not rest until she had eradicated every trace of it.

But even as she stood victorious on the field, a voice echoed in her mind, a voice she couldn't ignore: *This is just the beginning, Elara. They will come for you, and this time, you will be alone.*

With this, the story continues, unveiling the true cost of betrayal and the toll it takes on a leader's soul. Elara's resolve will be tested again and again, and every choice she makes will shape the future of her kingdom. The battle for the throne is far from over.

○ Sacrifices Made

The battlefield was eerily silent as the final confrontation loomed. The sky above, once bright and clear, now hung heavy with dark clouds, as if the heavens themselves sensed the weight of what was to come. Elara stood at the edge of the encampment, her armor reflecting the dim light of the encroaching storm, her thoughts tangled in a web of conflicting emotions. The air was thick with tension, and the distant hum of approaching forces was the only sound that dared to break the stillness.

For so long, she had carried the mantle of the Queen, bearing the hopes of her people, the dreams of a kingdom long divided by bloodshed and betrayal. But now, in this moment of truth, it was not her crown that weighed most heavily upon her, but the unbearable knowledge of what must be done to secure victory. There was no turning back.

Her mind flashed to the faces of those she had loved, those she had lost. She thought of Rhiannon, the powerful sorceress who had stood by her side from the beginning, her knowledge of ancient magic indispensable in the battles they had fought together. The bond they shared had been more than friendship—it was a sisterhood forged in fire and blood. Yet even Rhiannon had her price, one she had agreed to pay in exchange for the power that had helped them thus far.

Elara's heart clenched as she remembered the final words Rhiannon had spoken to her before disappearing into the shadows of the battlefield. "To win this war, Elara... to defeat the forces of darkness, you will have to give up everything you hold dear. Even your own soul, if necessary."

The sorceress had not been wrong. The ritual required to call upon the full strength of the bloodline, to awaken the ancient powers buried deep within Elara's veins, would demand a sacrifice far greater than any of them had anticipated. To defeat the Vanguard and its twisted leaders, Elara had to make a choice that no ruler should ever have to make. The cost of victory would be her humanity.

She could still feel the weight of that decision pressing down on her, the echoes of Rhiannon's warning haunting her thoughts. But there was no time for doubt, no time for regret. Her kingdom, her people, depended on her, and the darkness was closing in faster than she could outrun it.

The wind picked up, carrying the scent of impending rain. In the distance, the first flickers of lightning cracked the sky, illuminating the horizon like a signal of what was to come. Elara turned away from the storm, her eyes locking with those of her most trusted allies. Eamon, the seasoned general who had been by her side since the beginning of the uprising, nodded solemnly at her. His face was lined with exhaustion, but his resolve had never faltered.

"We stand with you, my queen," he said quietly, his voice a steady anchor in the storm of uncertainty.

Elara nodded in acknowledgment, but her thoughts were elsewhere. She knew what must be done, but the weight of the decision threatened to swallow her whole. She could not bear the thought of losing anyone else, of sending her people to their deaths in a war that seemed endless. And yet, the alternative was worse—if they failed now, the kingdom would fall, and all their sacrifices would have been in vain.

The battle began as the first wave of enemy forces charged forward, a sea of dark figures crashing against the walls of the encampment. Elara drew her sword, her grip tightening as she stepped onto the front lines. The familiar rush of adrenaline surged through her veins, but it did little to quell the storm within her heart.

In the midst of the chaos, her eyes found Rhiannon's figure, standing at the edge of the battlefield, her hands raised high, chanting incantations that could change the course of the fight. Elara knew that this was the moment. The moment when the ultimate price would be paid.

With a final, determined breath, Elara stepped forward, calling upon the ancient magic that coursed through her blood. She felt it surge within her, a power unlike anything she had ever experienced. It burned through her veins, consuming her from the inside out, but she did not flinch. She had made her choice.

The power exploded outward, a burst of raw energy that shattered the ground beneath her feet. The Vanguard forces recoiled in terror as the air around Elara crackled with power. But as the magic took hold, Elara felt herself slipping away, her body growing weaker, her sense of self fading.

She could hear the cries of her people, the screams of her soldiers as they fought to hold back the enemy. But their voices grew distant, fading into the background as the magic consumed her. She had given everything. And in the end, it was enough.

The Vanguard's forces crumbled before her, their strength shattered by the power of the bloodline. The battle was won, but at what cost?

As the dust settled and the storm clouds began to part, Elara collapsed to her knees, the weight of the magic leaving her broken and hollow. She had done what was necessary, but the price was a heavy one. The kingdom had been saved, but she had sacrificed herself in the process.

Her allies gathered around her, their faces filled with a mixture of awe and sorrow. Eamon knelt beside her, placing a hand on her shoulder.

"You've done it," he whispered, his voice thick with emotion. "The kingdom is safe."

Elara managed a faint smile, though it was laced with sadness. "I have saved them," she murmured, her voice barely a breath. "But at what cost?"

And as the first rays of sunlight broke through the clouds, Elara knew that the true cost of victory was still to be fully understood. The blood of the fallen, the sacrifices made, would forever haunt the kingdom she had saved. And she, too, would carry that burden for the rest of her days.

The dawn light seemed almost unreal, a cruel contrast to the darkness that lingered in Elara's heart. Her vision blurred as she gazed at the rising sun, the warmth of its rays doing little to chase away the chill that had settled in her bones. She had saved the kingdom, yes, but what kind of queen was she now? What remained of her humanity after the price she had paid?

Eamon remained at her side, his strong hands steadying her as she struggled to remain upright. The sounds of victory filled the air—cheers of soldiers, the clash of swords fading into silence as the last remnants of the enemy scattered. But for Elara, there was only the haunting weight of sacrifice.

"I have no words for what you've done, Elara," Eamon said softly, his voice thick with both admiration and grief. "You gave everything."

Her lips trembled, but she couldn't find the strength to respond. She had no answers for him, no comfort to offer. The burden of her choice, the true depth of the magic she had invoked, was still unraveling inside her. It was not just the toll on her body that she felt—it was the echo of Rhiannon's warning, the silent scream of a part of her soul that had been torn away.

The battle had ended, but the war within her raged on.

Rhiannon appeared then, stepping from the shadows of the battlefield like a specter. Her once radiant form was now faded, her eyes haunted by the same darkness that had claimed Elara's soul. Yet there was a quiet peace about her, as though she had come to terms with the cost of their choices.

"Elara..." Rhiannon's voice was gentle, yet there was an unmistakable edge to it, a shared understanding between the two women. "It is done. The magic you wielded, it was the only way."

Elara's eyes lifted to meet Rhiannon's, and for the first time in what felt like an eternity, she found herself searching for solace in the eyes of her friend. But there was no comfort to be found. Only the truth of their actions.

"I've lost something I can never get back," Elara whispered, her voice hollow. "I didn't think it would feel like this. I thought I was prepared for the consequences."

Rhiannon knelt beside her, placing a hand over Elara's heart, where the bloodline magic had once surged with power. The warmth of her touch was familiar, a fleeting reminder of the bond they had shared. "None of us are ever prepared, Elara. Not for the weight of the choices we must make. But you did it for them. For your people."

"But what of me?" Elara's voice cracked, the pain of her inner turmoil breaking free. "What remains of the woman who stood before you, who dreamed of a kingdom restored? What of the future I wanted?"

"There are no guarantees in this world, no promises of what the future will hold," Rhiannon said softly, her eyes meeting Elara's with a deep understanding. "But what you've done today... you've forged a future for them. And that is a gift, no matter the price."

Elara nodded weakly, but it felt like an empty gesture. She had indeed secured a future for her people, but at what cost? Her mind wandered to the faces of her loved ones—the allies, the soldiers who had fought alongside her, the family she had lost. They had all paid a price, but it was her soul that would be forever marked by this battle.

Eamon stood silently, his gaze fixed on the horizon where the remnants of the battle lay in ruin. "The kingdom will need you, Elara," he said, his voice firm with conviction. "Your strength, your leadership. There is still much to rebuild."

"I can't lead them like this," Elara murmured, her voice barely a whisper. "Not when I've given up so much of who I was. I'm not sure I can ever be the queen they need."

Rhiannon placed a hand on Elara's shoulder, her touch gentle but unwavering. "The queen they need is not the one who stood before the battle, but the one who emerged from it. You are stronger than you realize."

The words were meant to reassure her, but they only deepened the chasm within her heart. Strength. Was it truly strength to lose oneself in the pursuit of something greater? Was it truly strength to sacrifice everything for the survival of others?

The wind shifted, carrying with it the scent of the earth and the distant sound of the sea. It was a strange comfort to Elara, the reminder that life went on even after the storm had passed. But she was no longer the same woman who had set out to reclaim her kingdom. And perhaps, that was the true cost of victory: the irreversible transformation of the self.

As she stood, with Rhiannon and Eamon at her side, Elara knew the road ahead would be long. The kingdom was safe—for now. But she could not escape the knowledge that the war had not ended for her, not truly. The battle within her would continue to rage, its consequences following her like a shadow.

And yet, she would endure. For her people. For her kingdom. For the memory of those who had sacrificed everything to see the dawn of this new era.

But at what cost? The answer would come in time. For now, all Elara could do was walk forward into the uncertain future, carrying the weight of her choices, the echoes of sacrifice lingering in the air around her.

○ Power Shattered

The winds howled through the ruins of the battlefield, carrying with them the scent of blood and destruction. Elara stood at the edge of the once majestic fortress, now reduced to smoldering wreckage. Her eyes, normally a shade of steel and resolve, were now clouded with the weight of what had just transpired. The battle was over, but the cost had been far more than what she had anticipated. Victory had come at a steep price.

Her kingdom, the very foundation of which she had spent her life building, was on the brink of collapse. It was as if the very essence of power, once held so tightly in her hands, had now slipped through her fingers like sand. What was supposed to be a triumph over the forces that sought to tear her down had instead left her with a fractured empire and a broken spirit.

Elara's heart thudded painfully in her chest as she looked around at the bodies of fallen soldiers, allies, and enemies alike. The men and women who had fought beside her, who had pledged their loyalty, were now nothing more than lifeless shells. The war had been brutal, and even in victory, the bloodshed was undeniable. But there was something deeper gnawing at her — something that would not let her rest. The realization that the true enemy had never been on the battlefield, but rather in the shadows, had come too late.

She turned her gaze to the horizon, where the faintest glow of dawn began to rise, signaling the end of another chapter in her reign. The battle had been won, yes, but the war was far from over. The shattered remnants of her power weighed heavily on her, and for the first time in years, Elara questioned the very purpose of her struggle. Was it worth it? Was the price of victory too high?

As her thoughts swirled, a voice broke through the silence. Rhiannon, her most trusted advisor and confidante, stood by her side. Her presence was a quiet comfort, but Elara knew that even Rhiannon could not soothe the storm raging within her.

"Your Majesty," Rhiannon began softly, her voice carrying a note of sorrow, "the kingdom needs you now more than ever. You've won the battle, but the war of hearts is far from over. You must unite what's left, rebuild what's broken, and prove that power, though shattered, can be reforged."

Elara turned to face Rhiannon, her expression hardening. "I don't know if I can," she admitted, her voice barely above a whisper. "I thought that if I destroyed the enemy, I would finally find peace. But instead, I find that all I've done is destroy everything I worked for."

Rhiannon stepped closer, placing a gentle hand on Elara's arm. "Power is never easy to hold, my queen. It is a fragile thing, easily shattered. But it is also resilient. You have the strength to rebuild it. Not alone, of course. You'll need your allies, the ones who have stayed true to you. But you can do it. I know you can."

Elara's gaze softened as she looked at Rhiannon, the weight of her words sinking in. The truth was painful, but it was also a beacon of hope. Power had been shattered, but it wasn't gone. Not entirely. It could be reforged, rebuilt from the ashes, if she was willing to face the future with the same fire that had once led her to victory. The question was, could she? Would she?

As the first rays of the sun touched the blood-soaked earth, Elara made a vow to herself. The power she had lost would be reclaimed, not through violence or bloodshed, but through unity and vision. She would rebuild her kingdom. She would stand strong, no matter the cost.

The power was shattered, but it was far from broken.

As the days passed, Elara found herself at the crossroads of her past and future. The remnants of the battlefield were still fresh in her mind, but she knew that time was the enemy now. The people needed direction, hope, and a leader who could show them the way forward. What she had once considered to be her strength — her unyielding ambition — now seemed like a burden. Could she trust herself to lead when everything she had fought for was in pieces?

The echoes of her decisions weighed heavily on her shoulders, but it was the silence that followed her every step that disturbed her the most. The council had dispersed after the victory, each member retreating into their own corner of the kingdom, their minds clouded by uncertainty. Even Rhiannon, ever the stalwart adviser, seemed to have a shadow of doubt in her eyes.

Elara sat in her chambers, the walls closing in on her. She had made the choice to take the throne, to fight for a kingdom that was once her birthright. Now, however, that same throne seemed distant, its power hollow and fragile. She had defeated the enemy — but it was as if a part of herself had been defeated as well.

A knock at the door interrupted her spiraling thoughts. "Enter," she called, her voice hoarse. The door creaked open, revealing Aidan, her childhood friend and the captain of her most loyal guard. His presence always brought a semblance of comfort, but today, even his familiar face did little to ease the tension that gripped her heart.

"Your Majesty," Aidan began, bowing slightly before stepping forward. His eyes, dark and intense, never strayed from hers. "The people are starting to question the stability of the realm. There are whispers in the streets, rumors of rebellion stirring in the shadows."

Elara's stomach churned at the thought. Rebellion. Her greatest fear had come to life. The very thing she had fought to suppress had started to seep into the cracks of her shattered empire.

"Whispers?" she echoed, the weight of the word like a stone in her chest. "What kind of whispers, Aidan?"

"Calls for leadership," Aidan replied, his voice steady but his eyes betraying concern. "Many of the old houses are rallying their forces. They see an opportunity in your absence, in the cracks in your power. They want to take advantage of your weakness."

Elara's hands clenched into fists, the pain of betrayal sharper than any blade. She had fought so hard to protect this kingdom, to maintain order in the chaos. But the very people she had entrusted with her trust — her closest allies — now stood on the precipice of betrayal.

"I cannot let them tear this apart," she said quietly, her resolve hardening. "The kingdom is mine to lead, and I will not let it slip into the hands of those who would destroy it."

Aidan nodded, a quiet understanding passing between them. "Then we will fight, together. But you must understand, Elara, this is not just a battle for power. This is a fight for the soul of your kingdom. It is a war of hearts and minds, not just steel and blood."

Elara closed her eyes for a moment, allowing herself a breath. She had been focused so long on the external battles, the wars fought with weapons and armies, that she had forgotten the war within. The war that raged between loyalty and ambition, between the will to control and the need for unity.

"You're right," she murmured, her voice barely a whisper. "It's more than just a fight for power. It's about who we are, who we want to be. And if I am to rebuild what has been broken, I must first rebuild myself."

Aidan's gaze softened, and for a brief moment, Elara could see the woman she once was, the girl who had dreamed of a better world. Before the crown, before the battles, before the weight of the decisions that had torn her apart. There was a flicker of that spark left, buried deep beneath the layers of pain and loss.

But she could not afford to be weak. Not now. Not when everything was at stake.

"We will stand together," Elara said, her voice steady and resolute. "I will not let this kingdom fall. Not to rebels, not to traitors. It will rise again, stronger than before."

Aidan gave a single nod, a silent promise passing between them. He knew what was at stake. He knew what she had sacrificed to get to this point, and he understood that this next battle would be the one that would define her reign.

Elara's thoughts turned once more to the broken pieces of her power, scattered like fragments of a once magnificent sword. But even a broken sword could be reforged, if it was wielded with strength and purpose. And Elara would do whatever it took to rebuild the throne that had been shattered, to rebuild herself and her kingdom.

The power may have been shattered, but it was not beyond repair.

3. The Queen's Choice

- A Deal with Darkness

The moon hung low in the sky, casting an eerie silver glow over the vast, desolate plains. Elara stood at the edge of the ancient stone circle, her heart pounding in her chest. The wind whispered through the darkened trees, carrying with it the scent of rain and decay. In the distance, she could see the flickering of distant torches, the remnants of a once-glorious army now lost to the winds of time.

Before her stood a figure, cloaked in shadow, its presence both imposing and unnatural. Its form seemed to shift with the night, a silhouette that defied the very laws of nature. Elara's breath caught in her throat as she met the figure's cold, piercing gaze.

"You have come," the figure said, its voice a low, unsettling growl, like the sound of stone grinding against stone.

Elara's lips trembled, but she steeled herself. The weight of her kingdom's fate rested on this moment, this bargain that had been forged in desperation. Her kingdom teetered on the brink of collapse, its enemies closing in from all sides. The rebellion was stronger than ever, and the darkness that had long been sealed away threatened to rise once more. It was a darkness that called to her, a force she could neither understand nor control.

But control, she knew, was no longer an option.

"I have come to make a deal," she said, her voice unwavering despite the fear gnawing at her insides. "I seek the power to save my people. To protect them from what is coming."

The figure's lips curled into a wicked smile, revealing teeth that seemed too sharp, too cruel. "A deal with darkness, is it? You know the cost, don't you, Elara? Power such as this does not come freely."

Elara's pulse quickened. She had heard the legends, the whispered tales of those who had sought power and paid the ultimate price. Yet, standing here now, she felt the weight of her choices bearing down on her. There was no turning back. Her people were on the edge of destruction, and this was the only path left open to her.

"I am willing to pay whatever it takes," she replied, her voice steady despite the turmoil inside her.

The figure extended a long, skeletal hand toward her, its fingers twitching with anticipation. "Then you must give me what is most precious to you. Your heart, your soul, your very essence. In return, you will have the power to destroy your enemies, to reshape your destiny."

Elara swallowed hard, the gravity of the offer sinking in. Her heart—her soul—she had already given so much to this kingdom. Was there anything left to sacrifice?

"Your offer," she began, "is tempting, but what happens when the power you give me begins to consume me? What happens when I can no longer control it?"

The figure's smile widened, the shadows around it thickening as if feeding off her fear. "The power you seek will never be tamed. It will consume you, yes, but it will also give you strength beyond imagining. You will be more than a queen—you will be a goddess. The world will bend to your will. But there is a price. It always is."

Elara closed her eyes, feeling the cold winds whip around her. She could almost hear the cries of her people, their desperate pleas for salvation. She could feel the weight of their hopes, their dreams, and their fears pressing down on her like a mountain. This was not just her kingdom at stake; it was the future of all those who depended on her.

Taking a deep breath, Elara made her decision. "I will pay the price," she said, her voice fierce, determined. "I will do whatever it takes."

The figure nodded slowly, its eyes gleaming with malevolent satisfaction. "Then it is done."

In that instant, the air grew heavy with dark energy, the shadows around her growing deeper, more oppressive. Elara felt the power surge through her, burning like fire in her veins. She gasped as it coursed through her body, filling her with strength and knowledge she had never known before. It was a power unlike anything she had imagined, vast and uncontrollable.

But with it came a darkness—a hunger that gnawed at the edges of her soul, threatening to consume her entirely.

The figure stepped back, vanishing into the shadows as quickly as it had appeared. Elara stood alone in the stone circle, trembling as she felt the weight of her bargain settle upon her. She had made the deal. The darkness was now hers to wield.

But at what cost?

The wind howled around her as if warning her of the dangers that lay ahead. Elara stood in the center of the stone circle, her breath shallow and uneven. The air felt thick, suffocating, as though the very earth beneath her feet had become a battleground between the forces she had just invoked. Her heart pounded in her chest, and her hands trembled, not from fear, but from the overwhelming surge of power now coursing through her veins.

It felt as though the world had shifted, as though reality itself had bent around her will. Her mind was alive with the whispers of ancient voices, the faintest flicker of memories that were not her own. The knowledge came to her unbidden—strategies of war, forgotten magics, the deepest secrets of her enemies. She could feel the pulse of the land beneath her, the heartbeat of her kingdom, and it was alive with potential. But it was also hungry. Dark and ravenous.

The price was not simply the soul she had pledged, but the toll it would take on her spirit. Elara could already feel the subtle shifts, the way her thoughts twisted and darkened. Her once-clear purpose now seemed hazy, clouded by the very power she had sought to control.

But there was no turning back. She had chosen this path, and with it came a destiny she could not escape.

Her kingdom's survival depended on her—and on this power. She could feel the pull of it now, the call to reshape her world, to crush her enemies beneath her feet. She could taste the blood of the coming battles, the victories that would be hers to claim. But even as the thrill of triumph surged within her, a darker, more sinister thought whispered in her mind: *How long before the darkness consumes everything I am?*

Elara clenched her fists, forcing the thought aside. She could not afford weakness—not now, not when so much was at stake. Her kingdom, her people, they would rise again under her rule. She would not allow the past to define her fate. The rebellion would fall, the traitors would be silenced, and the ancient forces threatening her rule would be eradicated.

A voice echoed through her mind, faint yet insistent. *Remember your promise, Elara. You will become more than a queen. You will become the embodiment of power itself. But be careful, for power has a way of twisting those who seek it.*

The warning came too late. The darkness was already settling in, creeping into the very corners of her soul. Her body ached, as though every muscle was being pulled in different directions. She had never felt more alive, more powerful, and yet at the same time, she had never felt more vulnerable. The burden of what she had done was heavy—so heavy she could hardly bear it.

She took a step forward, her eyes scanning the night as if waiting for some sign, some guidance. There was nothing. Only the silence of the forest, the whisper of the wind, the weight of the power now bound to her.

Elara knew she had to act quickly. Her enemies were already moving, gathering strength. The rebellion's leader, the shadowy figure known only as The Serpent, was already making his move. His spies had infiltrated her court, sowing discord among her allies. And there were others—those who would stop at nothing to see her fall, to see the kingdom she had fought so hard to build crumble to dust.

With the power of the darkness now flowing through her, Elara knew she could crush them all. But at what cost? The question lingered in her mind, an echo of doubt that refused to fade. Would she lose herself in the pursuit of victory? Would the very darkness she sought to wield become her undoing?

There was only one way to find out.

With a final, steadying breath, Elara turned from the stone circle and began her journey back to her castle. The road ahead would be long, fraught with danger and deception, but she was no longer the woman she had been. She was something more—something darker. And with every step she took, the shadows at her back grew larger, swallowing the light.

The deal had been made. Now, Elara would learn whether the power she had gained would save her people—or destroy her.

○ The Ultimate Betrayal

The moon hung low in the sky, its pale light casting long shadows across the ruined landscape. The wind howled, carrying with it the stench of decay and the promise of doom. Elara stood on the edge of the battlefield, her eyes fixed on the horizon, where the dark silhouette of the enemy's fortress loomed. Her heart pounded in her chest, not from the exertion of battle, but from the gnawing sense of impending disaster.

She had trusted him. No, she had *relied* on him. Malor, once a loyal advisor, had been her closest ally. Together, they had fought to unite the fractured kingdom, to forge a future in which her bloodline could reign without the constant threat of assassination or revolt. But now, everything she had worked for seemed to crumble at her feet, as the weight of his betrayal settled upon her shoulders like an iron chain.

Elara could still remember the first time she had met Malor. He had been a humble warrior, a man of few words, but his eyes had held a fire she had admired. When he swore his allegiance to her, she had believed him—believed in his unwavering commitment to her cause. Over the years, he had become her most trusted confidant, her advisor in matters both political and personal. Together, they had navigated the treacherous waters of court intrigue, always one step ahead of their enemies. But now, it seemed that the man she had trusted more than anyone else had played her like a pawn.

Her thoughts were interrupted by the sound of footsteps behind her. She turned, her hand instinctively reaching for the dagger at her side, but it was not an enemy who stood before her. It was Malor.

His expression was unreadable, his once warm eyes now cold and distant. The air between them crackled with tension, thick with the weight of unsaid words. Elara's breath caught in her throat as she studied him. This was not the man she had known. This was something else entirely.

"Why?" she whispered, her voice breaking the silence. "Why would you do this?"

Malor's lips curled into a smile, but it was devoid of warmth. "You were always too trusting, Elara. Too blinded by your own ambitions to see the truth." He took a step closer, his presence oppressive, like a storm on the verge of breaking. "The kingdom you sought to build? It was never meant to be yours. You were just a means to an end."

Elara's heart ached as the weight of his words settled over her like a crushing wave. Her mind raced, trying to make sense of the betrayal, of the man who had once stood by her side now turning against her. But even as she struggled to understand, she knew one thing for certain: this was not just about power. This was personal.

"You were never loyal to me," she said, her voice low but steady. "You were only loyal to yourself."

Malor's smile faltered, but he did not deny her words. "I gave you everything. My loyalty, my trust, my blood. But you, Elara, you were never truly mine. You were always bound by your family's legacy, by the weight of your bloodline. You were never free."

Elara felt her pulse quicken as his words cut through her like a knife. She had spent her life fighting for her family, for the crown, but in that moment, she realized that everything she had believed in, everything she had worked for, had been a lie. The kingdom, the throne—it had all been a game, and she had been the pawn.

She swallowed hard, her throat tight with the bitterness of betrayal. "What do you want, Malor?" she asked, her voice barely above a whisper.

"I want what was promised to me," he replied, his voice cold and final. "The throne. The power that was rightfully mine from the beginning. And I will have it, one way or another."

Elara's hand tightened around the hilt of her dagger. The fire within her was rekindled, fiercer than ever before. She had been betrayed, but she would not let him destroy everything she had fought for. With a swift motion, she drew her weapon and lunged at him, the blade gleaming in the dim light.

But Malor was faster. In one fluid motion, he grabbed her wrist, twisting it painfully, forcing the dagger from her grasp. Elara gasped in pain, but she refused to yield. Her eyes burned with fury as she met his gaze.

"You think you can defeat me, Elara?" Malor sneered, his grip tightening. "You've already lost."

"Not yet," she spat, the defiance in her voice unwavering. "Not as long as I still breathe."

With a sudden surge of strength, she broke free from his grasp, launching herself at him once more. This time, her aim was true. She drove her knee into his chest, knocking him off balance, before sweeping his feet out from under him. As he stumbled back, Elara grabbed the dagger, her fingers closing around the hilt with a renewed sense of purpose.

Malor's eyes widened in surprise, but there was no fear in them—only a cold, calculating amusement. "You think this will change anything?" he asked, his voice a low growl. "The blood of the fallen will never stop haunting you."

Elara raised the dagger high, her heart pounding in her chest. For a moment, time seemed to stand still. She could feel the weight of every choice she had ever made, every life she had taken, every promise she had broken. And in that moment, she knew what had to be done.

With a swift motion, she drove the dagger into his heart.

Malor's body went limp in her arms, his life fading with the same ease as the night. Elara stood over him, her chest heaving with the effort of her struggle. She had won, but the victory felt hollow, the cost too high. She had lost more than she had gained, and the road ahead was uncertain. The ultimate betrayal had been dealt, but the kingdom she had fought so hard to protect now lay in ruins.

The weight of the throne, and everything it represented, pressed down upon her. But as the blood of her enemy stained her hands, Elara knew that the reckoning was far from over. The true battle had only just begun.

Elara stood there for a long moment, her breath coming in ragged gasps as she looked down at Malor's lifeless body. The knife still clutched tightly in her hand, its blade slick with blood, reflecting the pale light of the moon above. It was over. The man who had once been her closest confidant, the one she had trusted with her heart and her kingdom, was gone.

But as the weight of the moment pressed upon her, Elara couldn't shake the sense of emptiness that filled her chest. She had done what had to be done. Malor had betrayed her, manipulated her, and sought to claim everything that was hers. But the victory felt bitter. The price of this betrayal had been too high, and the echoes of his words reverberated in her mind like a cold whisper.

"The blood of the fallen will never stop haunting you."

Her eyes darted around the battlefield. The bodies of soldiers lay scattered across the ground, both friend and foe. The war that had raged for years, the battle that had seemed endless, had finally come to a conclusion, but the cost had been staggering. Too many had died, too many had sacrificed everything for a cause that now seemed hollow.

The throne, once the symbol of her family's power, now seemed more like a burden than a prize. Elara's bloodline had been built on betrayal and sacrifice. She had been born into this life, thrust into the cruel game of politics, a game where the rules were always shifting, and the stakes were life and death.

She wiped the blood from her hands, her fingers trembling, and turned toward the fortress in the distance. Her heart was heavy with the knowledge that the road ahead was uncertain. The kingdom had been saved, yes, but what was left for her now? Could she rebuild what had been broken? Could she trust anyone again?

As she walked away from Malor's body, her footsteps slow and deliberate, she could feel the eyes of her soldiers upon her. Their gazes were filled with admiration, but also fear. They had seen her destroy their former leader, a man who had once been hailed as a hero. What did that say about her? Was she any better than the man she had slain? Had she crossed a line that couldn't be uncrossed?

But Elara had no answers for them. She had no answers for herself. The only thing she knew for certain was that the war was not truly over. There were still factions vying for control of the throne, still enemies lurking in the shadows, waiting for their moment to strike. Malor's betrayal had been just the beginning.

And yet, in the quiet aftermath of the battle, as Elara stood alone among the ruins of her kingdom, she couldn't help but feel something stir deep within her—a flicker of hope. It was faint, fragile, but it was there. She had survived. She had taken the first step toward redemption.

But she knew the true test was yet to come. Rebuilding her kingdom would not be easy, and she would have to face the consequences of her actions. The road ahead would be treacherous, filled with enemies and allies alike who would test her resolve. But Elara was no longer the naive princess she once was. She had learned the harsh truths of power, betrayal, and survival.

And she would do whatever it took to rebuild her kingdom, to make it stronger than ever before—even if it meant making even more sacrifices along the way.

As she made her way toward the fortress, her thoughts turned to the future. She had a kingdom to reclaim, a throne to secure, and a legacy to restore. The ultimate betrayal had been dealt, but the true battle for her heart, for her kingdom, was just beginning.

The blood of the fallen would continue to haunt her, but Elara would carry it with her, as a reminder of the price of power—and the cost of loyalty. And with that burden heavy on her shoulders, she took her first step forward into the uncertain darkness of her future.

○ The Last Stand

The air was thick with the scent of smoke and blood. The battlefield stretched out beneath a blood-red sky, the horizon heavy with the promise of doom. Elara stood at the forefront of her forces, her dark cloak billowing in the wind, the weight of her crown pressing down on her like a thousand years of history. She could feel the pulse of her bloodline, the ancient power that flowed through her veins, and yet, it did little to ease the fear gnawing at her insides.

The Last Stand was upon them.

The enemy, once just a whisper in the dark, now loomed before her in full force, their armor glinting ominously in the dying light.

They were led by Vesper, the treacherous general who had once pledged loyalty to the crown. His betrayal had cut deep, and now he stood at the helm of a vast army, his eyes burning with a cold, unrelenting fury. His betrayal was personal. His hatred for her, for the throne, was as much about power as it was about revenge.

"Today, we end this," Elara muttered under her breath, the words lost in the wind but carrying the weight of an oath.

Beside her, her most trusted lieutenants stood in grim silence. Rhiannon, the fierce sorceress who had stood by her side through every trial, clenched her fists, the arcane energy crackling around her fingertips. A battle mage at her core, Rhiannon was the embodiment of wrath and control, a necessary ally in the war that had brought them to this moment.

And then there was Thorne. A man who had been both her closest friend and her most dangerous adversary. His loyalty was unwavering, but his past was dark—marked by choices that could have shattered their alliance had fate not been on their side. Today, however, there was no room for personal demons. The future of the kingdom rested on their unity.

Vesper's army advanced, a monstrous wave of steel and flesh, with no sign of mercy in their ranks. Elara's heart raced, her breath steady, as she raised her sword high. The crimson blade, passed down through generations, gleamed in the last rays of sunlight, a symbol of the crown's authority and the bloodshed it had caused.

"Charge!" Elara's voice cut through the air, sharp and commanding.

Her forces surged forward, an unstoppable force of fury and desperation. The clash of steel rang out as they collided with Vesper's army, the sound deafening, the ground shaking beneath the weight of their fury. Elara's heart pounded in her chest as she fought, her sword flashing through the air, each strike bringing her closer to the man who had once been her ally.

Through the chaos, she could see him—Vesper, standing tall amidst the carnage, his eyes locked on her. The battle between them was not just one of armies; it was one of wills, of the past, of betrayal. Every movement, every strike, was laced with the promise of vengeance.

Rhiannon unleashed a torrent of magic, a blinding wave of energy that tore through the ranks of Vesper's soldiers, sending them sprawling. The sorceress moved with a precision that only years of battle could refine, her power as lethal as any sword.

Thorne fought beside Elara, his movements calculated, his strikes deadly. He was the shadow in the midst of the storm, cutting down anyone who dared to approach the queen. Despite the blood and carnage surrounding them, there was a strange sense of calm in his eyes, a certainty that he would not fail her, no matter the cost.

But it wasn't enough. The enemy pressed on, overwhelming them with sheer numbers. Elara felt the weight of the battle shifting, the tide turning against them. The strength of her bloodline, the very power that had once brought her to the throne, felt distant now, slipping from her grasp like sand through her fingers.

In that moment of doubt, she saw Vesper break through the line, his figure rising above the melee. His eyes locked with hers, and for a fleeting second, there was a recognition in them—a shared understanding of the stakes, of the futility of the bloodshed that had brought them here.

"Elara," Vesper's voice rang out, cold and mocking. "You thought you could rule forever. But all kingdoms fall."

The queen's grip tightened on her sword, her resolve hardening. This was not just about a kingdom, a throne, or an empire. This was about her legacy, about the blood of her ancestors that had fought for this land, for this moment. And she would not let it slip away.

With a cry, she charged at Vesper, her sword raised high. The world around them blurred, the battle forgotten, as she closed the distance between them. The clash of their weapons was deafening, the sound of destiny itself ringing out across the battlefield. Blood flowed freely as their swords met, each strike a testament to the years of war, of sacrifice, and of loss.

The fight between them was brutal, raw, and unrelenting. Elara's strength was tested as never before, each strike from Vesper pushing her to her limits. But with every blow, with every clash, she found something deeper within herself—a power that transcended the bloodline, a will that was unstoppable.

Finally, with one last surge of strength, she drove her sword through Vesper's chest, his eyes wide with disbelief as he fell to the ground. The battlefield fell silent for a moment, the weight of his death settling over the land like a thick fog.

But the victory was bittersweet. The battle was far from over, and Elara knew that this was only the beginning of what would come next. The Last Stand had been won, but the price had been high. The kingdom was saved for now, but there were still enemies in the shadows, and the war was far from finished.

Elara stood alone amidst the carnage, her sword dripping with blood, her heart heavy with the knowledge that she had given everything to protect her people. And as the sun dipped below the horizon, she knew that the true reckoning had only just begun.

The battlefield was quiet now, but the silence was not peaceful. It was the eerie stillness that followed a storm, a pause before the next wave of violence. Elara's breath was ragged, her body battered and bruised from the relentless assault. Her fingers, slick with blood, tightened around the hilt of her sword. The weight of the victory was not one she could easily bear; the loss of so many, the faces of those who had fought and died for this moment, haunted her.

She turned slowly, surveying the aftermath of the battle. The ground was littered with fallen soldiers, both friend and foe, their lifeless eyes staring up at the sky. The stench of death mingled with the smoke, and the air was thick with the sounds of distant cries and groans. The cost of the Last Stand was too high, and the victory, though hard-won, tasted of ashes.

Rhiannon approached, her face pale, her hands still crackling with residual magic. The sorceress had been an unshakable force throughout the fight, her spells devastating the enemy ranks, but even she looked weary now. Her usually sharp features were softened by exhaustion, and the weight of the toll this battle had taken on her was visible.

"We did it," Rhiannon said, her voice heavy with a mix of relief and sorrow. "But at what cost?"

Elara didn't answer immediately. Her gaze lingered on the corpses scattered across the field, her thoughts a whirlwind of confusion and guilt. Vesper's body, still lying where it had fallen, seemed to mock her with its stillness. She had won, but it hadn't felt like a triumph.

"There will be no real victory until we rebuild," Elara finally said, her voice quiet but firm. "We must tend to the wounded, honor the dead, and prepare for what's to come. This war is not over."

Thorne, ever the silent observer, stepped forward, his face grim, his eyes filled with an unreadable emotion. His clothes were bloodstained, his expression dark and distant. Unlike Rhiannon, who had the ability to express her feelings through magic and words, Thorne's silence spoke volumes. His loyalty to Elara was unwavering, but the toll of battle had left scars that no one could see.

"The enemy may have fallen today," Thorne said, his voice low, "but Vesper was only the first of many who seek to destroy everything you've worked for, Elara. He was the blade, but there are others who will strike from the shadows."

Elara nodded, acknowledging the truth in his words. She had been prepared to face a world that resented her rule, but she hadn't expected it to be this cruel. The world was changing, and she was no longer sure if she could hold it together.

"The kingdom is fractured," she said, her eyes flickering toward the distant horizon where smoke still rose. "We've won the battle, but the war... it will never end. The nobility will rise against us, the factions will tear at the seams of what's left. We need allies, but who can we trust now?"

"We'll rebuild," Rhiannon said, determination creeping into her voice. "We'll fight for the people who still believe in you, who still believe in what you represent."

"And what is that, Rhiannon?" Elara asked, her tone sharp, but not unkind. "A queen on a throne of ash? A kingdom built on broken promises and blood?"

Rhiannon paused, then stepped closer, her hand resting gently on Elara's shoulder. "A queen who knows the cost of power, Elara. A queen who has faced the darkness and survived. That is what they'll need. Someone who is unbreakable."

Elara turned to face her, her expression softened. The bond they shared had always been one of strength, but now it was also one of understanding. They had both been tested in ways they had never imagined. They had seen too much to turn back now.

"I won't let this kingdom fall," Elara said quietly. "Not as long as there is breath in my body."

Her words were not empty promises. There was a fire in her that had not been extinguished, even after the bloodshed and the loss. She would not allow herself to be another ruler who crumbled beneath the weight of betrayal. She would stand tall, even if it meant standing alone.

The sky above them darkened, the last remnants of the sun vanishing behind the smoke and clouds. It was a fitting end to the day, and yet, Elara knew this was only the beginning. The real battle was yet to come.

"We will rebuild," she said, her voice firm, her heart heavy with the knowledge of the trials ahead. "But we must do it carefully. The ones who seek to destroy us will not stop. They will never stop. We must be prepared, and we must be stronger."

Thorne nodded, his eyes steady. "We will be."

The three of them stood together in the quiet aftermath, the weight of the world pressing down on their shoulders. The Last Stand had been fought and won, but it was only the first step in a much longer journey. The future of the kingdom depended on them now, and though the path ahead was uncertain, one thing was clear—Elara would not let her people fall. Not while there was breath in her body, not while her heart still beat with the fire of a queen who had survived.

As the darkness of night fell over the battlefield, they began to move. The war was far from over, but they would face whatever came next, together.

4. The Crimson Dawn

○ Elara's Victory

Elara stood at the edge of the battlefield, the once-impassable field now a vast expanse of broken earth, scorched remnants, and the fallen. The air was thick with the scent of smoke, blood, and death. The cries of victory were hollow to her ears, for she had won, but at what cost? The bodies of her enemies lay scattered across the land, but it was the faces of her friends, of her loyal soldiers, that haunted her thoughts.

Her heart, once fierce and unyielding, now felt heavy with the weight of leadership, of the countless lives lost under her command. She had driven the Vanguard back, their forces shattered, their plans destroyed—but the true cost of the war was yet to be counted. Elara's victory was a bitter one.

As the dust settled and the first light of dawn pierced the dark clouds that had hung over the battlefield like a grim shroud, Elara's gaze fell upon the ruins of her castle in the distance. Her kingdom, her people—everything she had fought to protect—lay in tatters. The rebuilding would take years, perhaps decades, but for the first time in a long while, there was a glimmer of hope.

Her thoughts turned to Rhiannon, the witch who had aided her in unlocking the ancient power within her bloodline, the power that had been key to their success. She had not only given Elara strength but had also bound herself to the queen in ways that neither fully understood. Now, the witch stood at her side, her expression unreadable, as always, but Elara could feel the change in the air. The witch had once been an ally in the shadows, but now... Now, there was a strange unease between them, a tension that neither could explain.

"Elara," Rhiannon's voice broke through her thoughts, soft yet sharp. "The battle is over, but the war is far from finished. The darkness that we fought off today is only a shadow of what is to come."

Elara turned to face her, the weight of her words sinking in. "I know. But for now, the kingdom is ours to rebuild, and we will do so. We must."

Rhiannon's eyes flashed with something unreadable. "Are you truly ready for what comes next? What this victory has cost you?"

Elara hesitated. Was she ready? Did she even know what it meant to be the ruler her people needed? Her strength had been tested, her resolve shattered, but now, as the blood of her enemies and allies alike soaked into the earth, she knew that she could not falter. The crown she wore was not just a symbol of power—it was a reminder that there was no turning back.

"I have no choice but to be ready," Elara said, her voice firm. "For if I falter now, if I let doubt take hold, then everything we've fought for will have been in vain."

The witch regarded her for a long moment before nodding, the tension easing ever so slightly between them. "Then let us see what you are truly made of, Queen."

Elara's gaze hardened as she surveyed the battlefield one last time. The future of the kingdom would depend on her decisions, on her leadership. But for now, in this fleeting moment, she allowed herself to feel the weight of her victory—bitter, but undeniable. It was hers.

The long road ahead would be fraught with challenges, with betrayals, with new enemies, and the ever-looming shadow of the Vanguard. But Elara had learned the cost of power. She had learned that a queen could not afford to be weak, not even in the face of her own doubts.

The blood that had been spilled today would nourish the soil of the kingdom's rebirth. The bones of the fallen would rise to remind them all of the price they had paid for peace.

And Elara, standing tall amid the ruins, would ensure that this victory would not be forgotten—not by her, and not by anyone who would dare threaten her people again.

The kingdom was hers to command. The last reckoning had been fought and won. But the story was far from over.

The air was still, but the ground beneath Elara's boots seemed to hum with a faint energy, a reminder of the ancient magic that had been awakened during the battle. She had felt it stir within her, an overwhelming force that surged through her veins, pushing her to the limits of her power. It had been that same power that had allowed her to defeat the Vanguard's greatest generals and shatter their ranks. But the cost had been more than just the lives of her enemies—it had come with a price she was only beginning to comprehend.

Turning from the battlefield, Elara strode toward the camp where her advisors and generals were waiting. The once-pristine tents now appeared war-torn, their fabric stained with the remnants of the conflict. The soldiers who had fought alongside her, who had believed in her cause, now stood in solemn silence, their faces weary but resolute.

At the center of the camp, her closest ally, Captain Rowe, awaited her with a look of deep concern in his eyes. His expression softened when he saw her, but there was an undeniable tension in the air between them. Rowe had been her right hand throughout this conflict, a loyal soldier whose skills in strategy and combat were unrivaled. Yet, as they stood in the wake of their victory, there was an unspoken question in the captain's gaze: What now?

"Elara," Rowe began, his voice low and strained, "you've won the battle. But the people... they're not celebrating. They're not rejoicing. They're frightened."

She knew he was right. There were no cheers from the soldiers, no triumph in the eyes of the citizens. Instead, there was fear. Fear of the future. Fear of what Elara's victory meant for the balance of power. The wars were not over; the enemies they had fought were only one piece of a much larger puzzle.

"I know," Elara replied, her voice tinged with sadness. "They've seen too much death, too much destruction. And I..." She faltered, looking away for a moment. "I've asked too much of them. Too much of myself."

Rowe took a step closer, his gaze softening. "You did what needed to be done. No one could have achieved what you've done. But you've made enemies, Elara. Enemies who will not forget. And you've made sacrifices that may come back to haunt us all."

Elara swallowed hard, feeling the weight of his words. She had done what she thought was necessary to protect her people, but in doing so, she had broken alliances, betrayed trust, and invoked ancient powers that had not been wielded in centuries. The consequences of her actions were still unknown.

"I have no illusions about the future, Captain," she said, her voice gaining strength as she faced the reality of her role. "But this kingdom will survive. We will rebuild, and we will rise again, no matter the cost."

Rowe studied her for a long moment before nodding. "I will stand by you, Elara. Always."

The weight of his loyalty brought her a small measure of comfort. As long as she had people like Rowe by her side, perhaps they could face whatever was coming next. But deep down, she knew that the true battle was not over. The Vanguard had been defeated, yes—but there were others in the shadows, waiting for their chance to strike.

"And what of Rhiannon?" Rowe asked, his voice quieter now.

Elara turned her gaze to the witch, who had been standing just beyond the camp, watching from a distance. Rhiannon had become a powerful ally, but also a constant source of uncertainty. The witch's motives were still unclear, her loyalty a complicated thing that Elara had yet to fully understand.

"I'll speak with her," Elara said, her voice steady. "There are things we need to discuss. Things that cannot be ignored any longer."

Rowe gave her a long look but said nothing. He trusted Elara, but even he had questions about the witch's growing influence.

As Elara made her way toward Rhiannon, the witch did not stir, her form outlined against the dimming sky. The silence between them was palpable, thick with unspoken words and the weight of their shared history. Rhiannon had helped Elara tap into the blood magic that had sealed their victory, but at what cost? The witch had warned Elara that power always demanded a price. Was the cost of this victory too great?

"Elara," Rhiannon's voice broke the silence, as cool and detached as ever, "we have much to discuss. You understand that this magic, this power, is not without consequence. It has changed you."

Elara looked at her, her heart heavy with the knowledge of the truth in Rhiannon's words. "I know," she replied, her voice strained but resolute. "But we've won. And that's all that matters. For now."

The witch studied her for a moment before nodding. "We shall see. Power has a way of making its demands. Be ready, Elara. There are forces out there that have yet to notice you've come into your own."

Elara met Rhiannon's gaze, the weight of the witch's warning sinking in. She had tasted victory, but she knew that the real battle was only just beginning.

○ The Kingdom Reborn

Elara stood on the balcony of the newly restored castle, her gaze drifting over the land below. The morning sun bathed the kingdom in a warm, golden light, but even its glow couldn't mask the weight of what had transpired in the past weeks. The kingdom had been reborn, but at what cost?

The once-beautiful kingdom, marred by bloodshed and betrayal, was now slowly recovering. Fields that had been burned, villages once left to rot in ruin, and towns devastated by the war were starting to heal, but the scars were still visible. Elara's heart felt heavy, knowing that the blood spilled in the name of power would forever stain the soil of her land. Yet, there was a spark of hope that flickered in her chest. The war was over. The traitors had been vanquished, and the threat of the Vanguard had been quelled, but the road ahead would not be an easy one.

Behind her, the sounds of her loyal council preparing for the day echoed through the corridors. She turned toward the door just as Rhiannon entered. The witch, once a mere whisper of a rumor, had become a close ally, her knowledge of ancient magic vital in their victory. Her eyes, though always distant, held a warmth that Elara had come to appreciate over time.

"Your Majesty," Rhiannon said, her voice soft but firm. "The people are starting to rebuild, but many are still uncertain. They need direction."

Elara nodded, her thoughts momentarily lost in the vast responsibilities that lay ahead. "What do you suggest?" she asked, turning to face the witch.

"We must offer them something more than just survival," Rhiannon replied, her eyes narrowing slightly as she spoke. "They need to feel the promise of something greater than the life they had before. Rebuilding the infrastructure is vital, but it is the spirit of the people we must address."

Elara understood the weight of Rhiannon's words. The kingdom might be physically restored, but it was the hearts of the people that needed healing. For too long, fear and oppression had ruled them. They had lived under the shadow of power that twisted the very core of their existence. To rebuild, they needed not only food, shelter, and security, but also a sense of hope—a vision for a future that did not repeat the horrors of the past.

"We will restore faith in our people," Elara said with resolve. "Not through empty promises, but through actions that show them that their suffering has not been in vain."

Rhiannon's lips curved into a rare smile. "I knew you would see it."

Elara turned back toward the land, watching as the people of her kingdom went about their work. There was no going back to the way things had been before. The past was a dark legacy that would never truly fade, but it was a part of them now—woven into the very fabric of the kingdom. They would move forward, but they would not forget.

As the day wore on, Elara made her rounds through the capital, meeting with leaders, workers, and soldiers. The streets were alive with activity—children running through markets, soldiers training for a future that, for now, seemed peaceful. Yet, Elara knew the calm would not last forever. The remnants of the Vanguard still lingered in the shadows, and old rivalries simmered beneath the surface.

But for today, she allowed herself a moment of peace. She had fought for this—fought for the kingdom's rebirth—and though the journey ahead would be fraught with challenges, it was a journey she was prepared to take. The kingdom was reborn, yes. But now, it was her responsibility to ensure it would never again fall to the darkness that once claimed it.

Her people, the true heart of the kingdom, were watching. And she would not fail them.

The afternoon sun cast long shadows over the stone streets as Elara walked through the capital. The bustling market was alive with activity, the scent of fresh bread mingling with the crispness of the morning air. Yet, despite the outward signs of recovery, Elara could not shake the gnawing feeling of unease that lingered in her chest. Every step she took was a reminder that the kingdom was not yet whole—at least, not in the way it should be.

Rhiannon had been right. The people needed more than just the tangible rebuilding of cities and infrastructure. They needed to believe in their future again, to feel as though they were more than just survivors of a past that haunted them. The challenge before Elara was not just to restore the land, but to restore the soul of her kingdom.

As she passed a group of children playing with scraps of cloth, laughter ringing in the air, her thoughts wandered to the past—before the war, before the betrayal that nearly destroyed everything. Her father had ruled with compassion, his word law and his heart just. Elara had always believed in the ideals he upheld, in the dream of a kingdom united by trust and loyalty. Now, she had to make that dream real, not just in the eyes of her people but in her own heart as well.

"Your Majesty," a voice interrupted her thoughts. Elara turned to see Prince Kaelen striding toward her, his expression as intense as ever. There was a weight in his eyes, a mix of responsibility and something deeper, something that had always lingered between them since the early days of the war.

"Prince Kaelen," Elara greeted, offering him a small nod. "What brings you to the streets today?"

His gaze swept over the crowds, his posture rigid, before he answered. "I've been overseeing the defense efforts, but I wanted to speak with you directly about something important. I fear we are not as secure as we would like to believe."

Elara's brow furrowed. "What do you mean?"

Kaelen's eyes hardened, and for a moment, she saw the shadow of the man he had been before the war—the soldier, the protector, the reluctant leader. "The remnants of the Vanguard are still out there. They have not disappeared. Our forces are spread thin, and rumors of unrest in the northern territories have begun to surface. We cannot afford to ignore this."

Elara sighed, her heart heavy with the weight of his words. The Vanguard had been defeated, yes, but its influence, its reach, was far deeper than they had anticipated. She had hoped that with the fall of their leaders, the organization would crumble entirely. But she had been wrong.

"How bad is it?" she asked, her voice steady but filled with concern.

Kaelen's jaw clenched. "We have reports of small skirmishes along the northern borders. And there are whispers that there are factions within the kingdom who still support their cause. We cannot be complacent."

Elara looked out over the kingdom, her gaze distant. The city may have been rebuilding, but the shadow of the Vanguard loomed over them still. She had to confront this threat, once and for all.

"Prepare the forces," she said, her voice hardening. "We will not let the remnants of the Vanguard tear this kingdom apart. It's time to eliminate them completely. I'll speak with the council and arrange for a swift response."

Kaelen nodded, his expression softening just slightly. "As you command, Your Majesty."

As he walked away, Elara's heart felt a mixture of dread and resolve. She had wanted peace, had fought for it with every ounce of her being. But peace was not a gift—it was something that had to be fought for, again and again. And the fight, it seemed, was far from over.

She turned back toward the castle, her mind whirling with the implications of Kaelen's words. The war had ended, but the battle for the future of her kingdom was just beginning.

○ The Legacy of the Bloodborn

Elara stood alone in the dimly lit chamber, her hand resting lightly on the cold stone of the ancient altar. The faint glow of candlelight flickered across the worn carvings that adorned the walls, depicting scenes of kings and queens long since lost to time. Yet, it was not their faces that haunted her thoughts, but the legacy of the bloodline she had been born into—a legacy that had bound her to a destiny she never asked for.

Her blood, thick with the power of the ancients, was both a blessing and a curse. She could feel the weight of it pressing down on her shoulders, an invisible chain that shackled her to the throne. The whispers of her ancestors echoed in her mind, their voices mingling with the growing unrest within the kingdom. The people murmured of rebellion, of the fading promise of peace, and Elara feared that the blood that flowed through her veins might be the very thing that destroyed everything she held dear.

For centuries, the Bloodborn had ruled, their power derived from an ancient pact made with dark forces long buried beneath the earth. It was said that each ruler of the Bloodborn dynasty bore the mark of their covenant—a symbol that had been passed down through the ages. Yet, as the years passed, the true nature of this pact had been forgotten, buried under layers of myth and legend.

Elara's mother had once spoken of it in whispers, warning her daughter of the price that came with the throne. "Power is not a gift, Elara," she had said, her eyes dark with the weight of knowledge. "It is a debt that must be paid. And your blood will be the currency."

Elara had never fully understood those words until now. The power she wielded, the ability to command armies and sway the hearts of men, was not born of her own strength, but from something older and far more dangerous. The blood that ran through her veins was not simply royal; it was cursed. And with each passing day, that curse seemed to tighten its grip on her, pulling her further from the woman she once was and closer to the monster she feared becoming.

As she gazed at the altar, her thoughts turned to the prophecy that had been passed down through generations. The one that spoke of the final ruler of the Bloodborn, the one who would either break the chain of darkness or fall victim to it. Elara's heart clenched in her chest. The prophecy had always seemed distant, a thing of stories and warnings. But now, it felt real—too real.

The ancient texts had always been vague about the prophecy's true meaning, but one thing was clear: the Bloodborn line would end with her. Whether she would be the savior or the destroyer, only time would tell.

Her mind raced as she thought of the choices ahead of her. The kingdom was on the brink of war, and the forces that sought to overthrow her were growing stronger with each passing day. The Bloodborn had long been a symbol of strength, but their enemies were no longer content with mere rebellion. They wanted to erase the legacy of the Bloodborn, to destroy the very foundation upon which the kingdom was built.

But how could Elara fight against the very thing that gave her power? How could she destroy the bloodline that ran through her veins, that had shaped her into the ruler she was?

A knock at the door broke her reverie, and Elara turned sharply. Her most trusted advisor, Alistair, entered, his expression grim. "Your Majesty," he began, his voice low, "the council has requested your presence. They... they wish to discuss the future of the kingdom."

Elara nodded, her mind still swirling with the weight of her legacy. The future of the kingdom was a fragile thing, held together by the delicate balance of power and fear. She had long known that her reign would be tested, but she had never anticipated it would be tested by her own bloodline.

With a deep breath, Elara turned away from the altar. "Tell them I will be there shortly."

As she left the chamber, she could feel the pull of her legacy tightening, its influence reaching out to claim her once more. The blood of the ancients was calling, and whether she answered or resisted, it would shape the fate of the kingdom.

For Elara, the true battle was not one of armies or political intrigue. It was a battle for her soul.

Elara's footsteps echoed through the empty halls of the castle, each one reverberating with a weight she couldn't escape. The walls, once familiar and comforting, now seemed to close in on her, as if the very stone itself whispered of the legacy she was born into. The air was thick with the scent of old parchment and dust, the remnants of an ancient past that clung to every corner of the palace.

As she entered the council room, the murmur of hushed voices fell silent. The nobles, high-ranking generals, and advisers all turned to face her, their eyes filled with a mixture of expectation and fear. They had seen the signs—the signs of weakness in her reign, the slow unraveling of the empire her ancestors had forged. They had felt the instability that the prophecy had predicted, the feeling that the end of the Bloodborn was nearing.

The weight of their gazes pressed on Elara as she took her seat at the head of the table. For a moment, no one spoke. The silence stretched between them like a fragile thread, and Elara could almost hear the collective breath of the room held in suspense.

Finally, Lord Eldric, the eldest member of the council, cleared his throat. His voice was thick with authority, but there was a tremor beneath it that betrayed his concern. "Your Majesty," he began, "we are at a crossroads. The rebellion grows bolder by the day. Our borders are no longer secure, and whispers of a new ruler, one not bound by the Bloodborn legacy, spread like wildfire through the kingdom."

Elara's fingers tightened on the armrests of her chair, her knuckles white. She had expected this, of course. The rebellion had been brewing for years, fueled by the same discontent that had plagued every dynasty before hers. But now, with the prophecy looming over her head, it felt different—more desperate, more urgent.

"And what do you propose we do about it?" she asked, her voice steady but laced with a cold edge. She had no patience for hesitation or indecision. If there was one thing she had inherited from her ancestors, it was the unwavering will to lead, even if it meant making difficult, impossible choices.

Lord Eldric exchanged a look with the others around the table, as if weighing his words. Finally, he spoke again. "We must strike at the heart of the rebellion. We cannot allow it to grow any further, or the kingdom will fall into chaos. There are those within the council who believe we should rally the armies and crush the insurgents, once and for all."

A murmur of agreement rippled through the room, but Elara held up a hand to silence them. Her mind raced, considering the implications of such a move. War, bloodshed—it was what her ancestors had been known for, but it was also what had led to their downfall. The legacy of the Bloodborn was one of conquest, of power gained and lost in the blink of an eye. She had always known that this moment would come, but the weight of it was heavier than she had imagined.

"No," Elara said, her voice sharp. "War will only feed the flames of rebellion. We need to understand what drives them, not just crush them. There are deeper currents at play here, currents that we have overlooked for far too long."

Her gaze swept the room, locking eyes with her most trusted advisors. "I will not be remembered as the queen who destroyed her people to save her throne. If we are to survive, we must first understand why they are rising against us. We will find the truth, no matter where it leads."

The council room fell silent again, the weight of her words hanging heavy in the air. Some of the nobles shifted uncomfortably in their seats, clearly unsettled by her decision. But others, those who had always admired Elara's intellect and cunning, nodded in agreement. They knew that her path was risky, but it was also the only path that had any hope of preserving the kingdom in the long run.

Alistair, her most trusted advisor, spoke then, his voice low and measured. "Your Majesty, I will gather information. We will learn who is truly behind this rebellion, and why it has grown to this point. But you must be prepared, Elara. What we uncover may be darker than anything we have imagined."

Elara nodded, her resolve hardening. "I am prepared. This kingdom will not fall to the will of those who would see it burn. I will not let the blood of my ancestors be spilled in vain."

As the council adjourned, Elara stood and walked to the balcony overlooking the kingdom. The sun was beginning to set, casting long shadows over the land. The world was changing, and she could feel it deep in her bones. The winds of destiny were shifting, pulling her toward a future she could not control.

But she would not go quietly. The legacy of the Bloodborn, for all its darkness, would not define her. She would write her own story, no matter the cost. And in the end, she would either break the chain of blood that bound her, or she would become its final victim.

Only time would tell which path she would choose.

Epilogue: A New Dawn

- The Future of the Kingdom

The air was thick with anticipation as Elara stood at the edge of the great balcony, gazing out over the sprawling kingdom she had fought so fiercely to protect. The once-crumbling walls of the castle now gleamed under the morning sun, a symbol of the strength that had risen from the ashes. The kingdom was no longer the fragile state it had been just a few short months ago. Its heart had been healed, its wounds mended, but the scars would remain forever.

The war was over, but the real battle had only just begun.

Elara's mind drifted back to the choices she had made, the sacrifices she had endured. She had lost so much along the way—trusted allies, dear friends, and even parts of herself. Yet, in the end, she had emerged victorious. The dark forces that once threatened to consume everything had been vanquished, their whispers silenced by the bloodshed of those who stood beside her. The old world was gone, and with it, the shadows that had ruled for centuries.

But what came next? The question hung heavily in the air, unanswered. The kingdom was free from its oppressors, but the future was an uncharted path, a landscape both beautiful and terrifying in its uncertainty.

Elara's thoughts were interrupted by the soft sound of footsteps behind her. She turned, her eyes meeting the calm gaze of Rhiannon, her most trusted advisor. The witch's presence was always a comfort to her, a reminder of the bond they shared through their trials and triumphs.

"The kingdom will need guidance," Rhiannon said, her voice steady yet carrying an unspoken weight. "The people will look to you for leadership, not just as their queen, but as a symbol of their hope. You've won their loyalty, Elara, but now you must show them what that loyalty means."

Elara nodded, her gaze drifting once more to the horizon. There was still much to rebuild. The old alliances had been shattered, but new ones had been forged in the heat of battle. She had to unite the fractured lands, heal the rifts between the various factions, and ensure that the power she wielded was not a curse, but a force for lasting change.

"How do I begin?" Elara asked quietly, her voice carrying the weight of a burden only she could truly understand.

Rhiannon stepped closer, her eyes softening with understanding. "Start with trust. The people need to know they are not forgotten. Rebuild the councils, restore the order that was lost. But do not forget what you have learned. Power can be a dangerous thing. Use it wisely, Elara."

The words were a warning, but also a reminder. Elara had seen firsthand how easily power could corrupt, how the line between justice and tyranny could blur when one was blinded by their own desires. She could not allow herself to become what she had fought so hard to destroy.

As she looked out over the kingdom, Elara felt a deep resolve settle in her chest. She would not fail her people. The road ahead would not be easy, and there would be challenges she could not yet foresee. But she was ready. She had to be. For the future of the kingdom, for the legacy of those who had fallen, and for the generations yet to come, Elara would lead with wisdom, compassion, and a relentless will to ensure that the kingdom's future would be brighter than its past.

The sun dipped lower in the sky, casting a golden light across the land. The kingdom was alive, and its heart still beat strong. But now, it was Elara who would determine the direction it would take. She stepped away from the balcony, ready to begin the next chapter of her reign.

The future of the kingdom rested in her hands.

As Elara descended the steps from the balcony, her mind raced with the weight of the decisions that lay ahead. She could hear the distant murmurs of the court below, the chatter of nobles and commoners alike, all eagerly awaiting her next move. The castle was alive with preparations, the scent of food filling the air, and the clattering of armor from the soldiers who still stood watch. The people were ready for change, hungry for something new, but there was a fine line between delivering that change and disrupting the delicate balance they had fought so hard to restore.

When Elara entered the grand hall, her eyes swept over the gathered councilors. The faces that had been with her through the darkest times now watched her with a mix of hope and apprehension. Among them was Lord Aldric, once a foe, now a trusted ally. His loyalty, earned through battle and sacrifice, was invaluable, but Elara knew better than to take it for granted. Trust was a fragile thing.

"My queen," Aldric said, stepping forward as she approached the head of the table. "The council is ready to begin."

Elara nodded, taking her seat. The weight of the throne, both literal and symbolic, was never lost on her. She could feel the eyes of her people, the pressure of their expectations, and the ever-present shadow of the past. But she would not allow fear to dictate her actions.

"We must rebuild," she began, her voice calm yet unwavering. "The kingdom is in ruins, and it is our duty to ensure it does not fall apart again. We will restore the councils, strengthen our alliances, and create a new order based on unity, not division. But we will do so with caution."

Her words hung in the air, heavy with meaning. This was not just about restoring what had been; it was about creating something better, something sustainable. Elara knew that if she did not act swiftly and decisively, the remnants of old power would rise again, eager to reclaim what they had lost. And there would be those who would seek to exploit the kingdom's vulnerabilities, both from within and beyond its borders.

"Lord Aldric," Elara continued, "you and your forces will remain at the borders. We need our defenses stronger than ever, and your experience in battle will be invaluable. Lord Varrick, I want you to oversee the rebuilding of the villages. The people need to know we have not forgotten them."

Aldric bowed, his expression steely, while Lord Varrick nodded in agreement. "Of course, my queen. We shall see to it at once."

"Rhiannon," Elara turned to her trusted advisor, "I need you to work with the remaining mages. We must secure the magical wards that protect the kingdom, and I want the council of elders to be established once more."

Rhiannon met her gaze, her eyes full of understanding. "It will be done, Elara. But we must be careful. The magical forces we've harnessed are powerful, and some may seek to use them for darker purposes."

"I trust you to keep them in check," Elara replied firmly. "The kingdom's future depends on it."

As the meeting progressed, Elara listened to the reports and recommendations of her councilors. There were many challenges to face, from food shortages in the outlying regions to the delicate matter of foreign diplomacy. Allies would need to be secured, but old enemies would have to be handled with care. The political landscape had shifted, and Elara had no illusions about the complexities of the new world she would navigate.

But even as she sat there, surrounded by her loyal supporters, a gnawing doubt lingered in the back of her mind. The kingdom was fragile, held together by a tenuous thread of hope and fear. She had done everything in her power to ensure victory, but the price had been steep. Now, she had to ensure that the same forces of darkness that once tore the kingdom apart would never rise again.

"One final thing," Elara said, her voice gaining strength as she looked around the room. "We must not forget the past. We cannot erase the bloodshed, the betrayal, and the suffering that has shaped us. But we can use it to fuel our resolve. This kingdom will not fall into chaos again. We will rise, together."

Her words, though heavy, were filled with conviction. The room was silent for a moment, the weight of her statement settling over the council like a storm. Elara knew that she could not do this alone. She would need the loyalty of each and every one of them. And yet, deep down, she also knew that the greatest challenge she faced was not the kingdom's external threats, but the fight for her own soul.

The path ahead was uncertain, but Elara would face it with the same strength and determination that had carried her through the darkest days. The kingdom's future was hers to shape.

- A Hopeful Beginning

The sun's first rays broke through the thick clouds, casting a warm, golden light over the kingdom. The war, which had torn the land apart for so long, had finally ended. The bloodshed and betrayal, the alliances forged and broken, now seemed like a distant memory, a nightmare that was slowly fading into the past. But even in this calm, there was an undercurrent of tension.

Elara stood on the balcony of her castle, gazing out over the sprawling lands that stretched before her. The horizon was dotted with the faintest signs of life, a few villagers already tending to their fields, the smoke from chimneys curling up into the sky. It was a new day, a new beginning. Yet the weight of what had been lost still hung heavy in the air.

Her thoughts drifted back to the days before the final battle, when she had made the choice that would change everything. It had been a decision fraught with consequences, but one that had been necessary. She had chosen her people over her own desires, sacrificing more than she cared to admit. The crown, the throne—none of it mattered when weighed against the lives of those she had sworn to protect.

Now, as the dust settled and the smoke of war cleared, Elara knew that the hardest part was still to come. Rebuilding the kingdom would take more than just strength and resolve—it would take healing. The scars left by years of conflict would not fade overnight. Trust had been shattered, and it would take time to rebuild the relationships that had once held the kingdom together.

She turned away from the balcony and walked through the quiet halls of the castle, her footsteps echoing softly. The sounds of the bustling castle grounds outside were muted within these walls, where silence had reigned for so long. But now, there was a sense of renewal in the air, a feeling that things could, and would, change.

As she reached the war room, she found her closest advisors waiting. Rhiannon, the witch who had stood by her side through it all, and Aric, the captain of her guards, were already deep in conversation. Their faces were weary, but there was something else—hope, a glimmer of something new.

"Your Majesty," Aric greeted her with a bow, though his tone was less formal than it once had been. "We've received word from the eastern provinces. The villages there are beginning to rebuild, and trade is starting to resume. There's much work to be done, but it's a good start."

Elara nodded, her eyes filled with quiet determination. "We'll need to act swiftly. The people need to feel that this new era is one of peace, not just in words, but in action. We cannot afford to falter now."

Rhiannon stepped forward, her expression thoughtful. "There are whispers of unrest in the north, though. Small pockets of resistance, loyal to the old regime, still remain. They will not simply disappear."

Elara's gaze hardened. "I will not let the shadow of the past follow us any longer. We will crush any remnants of the old ways, but we will do so with caution. The kingdom needs stability, not more bloodshed."

As they discussed the challenges ahead, Elara couldn't shake the feeling that the hardest battles were not yet over. The war had ended, yes, but the true test of her reign was just beginning. The people would look to her for guidance, for hope. She could not afford to fail them.

The decisions ahead would be difficult, and the path to peace would not be easy. But for the first time in a long while, Elara felt something she hadn't dared to believe possible: hope. A sense that, perhaps, the kingdom could rise from the ashes, stronger and united. The road ahead would be long, but with every step, there was a possibility of something better.

And in that quiet, uncertain moment, Elara made a vow to herself. No matter the cost, she would fight for this new beginning. For the kingdom, for her people, and for the future. She would ensure that the sacrifices made in the name of peace would never be forgotten, and that the legacy of the Bloodborn would endure for generations to come.

This marks the beginning of a new era, the start of Elara's reign as she seeks to heal the wounds of the past and forge a future for her people.

As the days passed, the weight of Elara's newfound hope began to settle in her bones. It was not an easy thing to hold onto, not after so much loss, but she found that she couldn't let go. The war had taken everything from her—the lives of friends, allies, even the innocence she had once taken for granted—but it had also forged something stronger within her. She had seen the depths of cruelty, but she had also seen the depths of sacrifice, and in that, she found something worth fighting for.

Her first test came sooner than expected. News arrived from the northern provinces—word of a band of insurgents, still loyal to the fallen regime, making their way through the rugged mountain passes. They were small in number, but they were well-equipped and dangerous. These weren't the remnants of the old army, but rather a collection of mercenaries and radical sympathizers who had never accepted her rule. If allowed to gain momentum, they could reignite the flames of war.

Elara knew she couldn't allow that. The kingdom needed peace, but more than that, it needed order. The last thing she could afford was another battle, especially one that could threaten the delicate fabric of unity she was so desperately trying to weave.

She gathered her council, her most trusted advisors. Aric stood at the head of the table, his brow furrowed in concentration as he spread out a map of the northern territories. "We've tracked their movements," he said, his voice steady despite the tension in the air. "They're well-hidden, but they're coming from the mountains. We can intercept them before they get too far into the valley."

Rhiannon, standing to the side, glanced up from the scroll she was studying. Her eyes glinted with a mixture of concern and curiosity. "I can feel them," she said softly, as though the words were an echo of something deeper. "Their presence is... unnatural. Dark magic lingers around them, something that should have died with the old regime."

Elara's heart tightened at the mention of dark magic. It was a force she knew all too well—the kind of power that could twist even the most noble hearts into monstrous things. It was the very thing that had kept her kingdom locked in chains for so long. She couldn't afford to let it return, not now, not when they were so close to beginning anew.

"I'll go with Aric," Elara declared, her voice firm. Her decision was met with a brief silence, the weight of her words hanging in the air. "We can't afford to let this group grow any stronger. I need to see it done, with my own eyes. We'll strike before they can spread their influence."

"Your Majesty—" Rhiannon began, but Elara held up a hand, silencing her.

"I know the risks, Rhiannon," Elara said, her tone resolute. "But I cannot afford to wait any longer. If we allow them to grow unchecked, we risk everything we've worked for."

With that, the decision was made.

The northern roads were treacherous, winding through narrow passes and dense forests, but Elara and her companions were no strangers to danger. They rode hard, cutting through the mountain terrain with the precision of those who had spent years on the battlefield. The air grew colder as they ascended higher, and the landscape grew more barren, the trees twisted and gnarled like the forgotten spirits of the land.

Night fell as they reached the last ridge before the valley. The campfire crackled in the darkness, and Elara stood apart from the others, gazing at the stars above. They had come so far, and yet she felt the weight of the decision pressing down on her more than ever. Was this truly the path to peace, or had she simply traded one war for another?

Aric approached, his expression unreadable in the firelight. "We'll strike at dawn," he said, his voice low and steady. "The insurgents are holed up in a cave not far from here. We'll move quickly, neutralize them before they can react."

Elara nodded, but her mind was far from the plan. Her thoughts drifted to the future of her kingdom, to the people who depended on her. Could she continue to be the queen they needed, or would her actions push them further from the peace they craved?

In that moment, Rhiannon joined them, her eyes dark with something that Elara couldn't quite place. "There's more at play here than we realize," Rhiannon said softly, almost as if speaking to herself. "This darkness—it's not just the old regime's remnants. Something far older is stirring. I can feel it."

Elara's heart skipped a beat. She turned to face the witch. "What do you mean?"

Rhiannon met her gaze, her eyes haunted. "There are forces at work in this land that have slept for centuries. We've only just begun to uncover the surface of what's truly happening. This insurgency—it's not just about politics. It's about something darker. Much darker."

The air around them seemed to thrum with a subtle energy, as though the very earth beneath their feet was aware of the approaching conflict. Elara couldn't shake the feeling that she was being pulled into something much larger than herself, something that would shape not only the future of her kingdom but the fate of the entire world.

"We'll deal with it," Elara said, her voice a mixture of resolve and uncertainty. "But first, we need to stop them."

With that, they prepared for the battle ahead. But in the back of Elara's mind, she couldn't help but wonder—what had Rhiannon felt, and what dark forces had begun to stir once more? Would this be the beginning of something far more dangerous than any of them could foresee?

The story moves forward, but the shadows of the past, and the stirrings of something far darker, loom large over Elara's every decision. The hope she had embraced was now being tested, not only by the remnants of the old regime but by a threat that no one could yet understand.

- The End of an Era

The sun was beginning to dip beneath the horizon, casting a reddish glow over the land that had long been shrouded in conflict and uncertainty. Elara stood atop the palace balcony, her gaze fixed on the horizon, where the once-foreboding silhouette of the city now seemed to glow with a newfound peace. It was the end of an era, but also the beginning of something uncertain, something that would require all her strength, wisdom, and resolve.

The war had taken its toll on the kingdom. The skies had been filled with the smoke of battle, the air thick with the tension of those who had fought, bled, and lost their loved ones. But now, as Elara looked out over the kingdom she had fought so hard to protect, there was a strange, almost unsettling calm. The darkness that had once threatened to consume everything was receding, but the scars it left behind would not fade so easily.

Behind her, the throne room was quiet. The once grand hall, now filled with the echoes of lost hopes and whispered betrayals, had witnessed the rise and fall of countless rulers. Elara's ancestors had sat upon this throne, their bloodline intertwined with the very fate of the kingdom. But with her victory over the Vanguard and the final battle against the forces that had long sought to tear the realm apart, Elara knew that she could not rule as they had. The world had changed, and with it, so too must the throne.

"Is it truly over?" The voice came from behind her, soft but carrying a weight of its own. Rhiannon, her trusted confidante, stood in the doorway, her face a mixture of relief and exhaustion. She had been by Elara's side through every battle, every dark moment, but even she knew that this victory had cost them both more than they had ever anticipated.

Elara didn't answer immediately. Instead, she allowed herself a long, quiet breath, letting the silence of the moment settle around her. "It's over for now," she finally said, her voice steady but laced with a weariness that had become familiar in recent days. "But the end of an era doesn't always mean the end of what came before."

Rhiannon stepped closer, her eyes searching Elara's face. She had watched her queen transform over the course of the war—once a ruler who had struggled with doubt and fear, now a woman hardened by loss, yet unyielding in her commitment to her people. "What will become of us now?" she asked, her tone tinged with both curiosity and concern.

"The kingdom... it's in your hands, Elara. The balance has shifted, but can you hold it?"

Elara turned to face her, her expression softening, but only slightly. She had seen the toll the war had taken on those closest to her, and she knew that even in victory, there were no guarantees. The road ahead was fraught with challenges, both internal and external. The bloodshed, the power struggles, the alliances built on fragile trust—all of it had to be dealt with, one piece at a time.

"I don't know," Elara admitted. "But I will try. I have to."

Rhiannon nodded, accepting the weight of her queen's words. The silence between them stretched for a long moment, filled only with the sounds of the distant city, the soft wind, and the fading light.

"Will you ever be able to let go of the past?" Rhiannon asked quietly, almost as though speaking to herself.

Elara's eyes flickered toward the horizon again. The past had shaped her, had forged her into the leader she was today, but it had also left her with scars that no amount of victory could ever truly heal. "Maybe not," she replied, her voice barely above a whisper. "But I've learned that I don't need to carry it alone anymore."

It was a small admission, but it held great meaning. Elara had been a queen who had fought against her own fears, against the very bloodline that had once promised her power but left her with nothing but the weight of expectation. And now, as she stood at the edge of this new era, she realized that it wasn't just her fate that was at stake—it was the fate of her people, her kingdom, and the world she had fought to protect.

The end of an era was not a clean break. It was a transition, a delicate balance between what had been and what could be. And as Elara watched the first stars begin to twinkle in the darkening sky, she felt the weight of that future settling into her bones. It was a future she would face with strength, yes, but also with the humility that came from knowing just how fragile that peace could be.

This marked the end of an era, but in many ways, it was only the beginning of a new chapter.

From the Author

AS I WRITE THE FINAL chapter of the *Bloodborn Chronicles*, I find myself reflecting on the journey that began with the rise of a single queen, whose courage and strength have shaped the fate of a kingdom. From the moment Elara first set foot on the path of power, her destiny intertwined with the bloodline of the ancients, a legacy both cursed and sacred, pulling her into a struggle far greater than herself. The echoes of that struggle have resonated through every page of this saga.

In *The Bloodborn Chronicles: The Last Reckoning*, we reach the culmination of a story that spans generations, battles, alliances, and betrayals. It is a tale of survival, of those who fight not just for the crown, but for the future of their people. But it is also a story of the choices we make when faced with the impossible—of those moments when the weight of responsibility becomes a burden too heavy to bear.

Elara's journey is one of transformation. She begins as a reluctant queen, haunted by the blood that flows through her veins and the power that threatens to consume her. But in the face of mounting darkness, she must evolve—confronting her deepest fears, testing her alliances, and discovering the true cost of power. Her path is not without sacrifice, and as the final battle looms, she must decide whether to embrace her destiny or reject it altogether.

This book, like the others in the *Bloodborn Chronicles*, is not simply about war or politics; it is about what it means to be human in the face of overwhelming forces. It is about love, loss, hope, and the search for redemption. It is about the shadows that dwell within all of us, and the light that we must sometimes fight to see.

To the readers who have followed Elara's journey from the beginning, thank you for your unwavering support. Your passion for these characters has been the fuel for my own, and I am grateful for every word of encouragement, every message, and every moment spent in this world together. For those who are new to the series, welcome. You are about to witness a conclusion that will leave you breathless, but one that I hope will also leave you with a sense of resolution and a deeper understanding of the power of choice.

As you turn the pages of *The Last Reckoning*, know that this is more than just an ending—it is a new beginning, both for the characters we have come to love and for the world they inhabit. The threads of their stories may be tied, but the legacy they leave behind will echo for generations to come.

May you find yourself captivated by the journey, and may the stories of the *Bloodborn* live on long after the final page has been turned.

With gratitude and honor,

Dorian Vale

Part I: The Awakening of Shadows

   1. The Queen's Descent
   2. The Betrayer's Whisper
   3. The Crimson Court
   4. A Legacy of Blood

Part II: The Rise of the Fallen

   1. Vanguard's Return
   2. The Witch's Mark
   3. Into the Abyss
   4. Alliances of Blood

Part III: The Final Reckoning

   1. The War of Shadows
   2. The Price of Power
   3. The Queen's Choice
   4. The Crimson Dawn
Epilogue: A New Dawn

www.ingramcontent.com/pod-product-compliance
Ingram Content Group UK Ltd.
Pitfield, Milton Keynes, MK11 3LW, UK
UKHW040726210325
456568UK00001B/75